I0623742

DEEP SPACE BOOGIE

WARP RIDERS 1

SCOTT BARON

Earth is the nest, the cradle, and we'll move out of it.

— Gene Roddenberry

CHAPTER ONE

Captain Sadira Perez sat at attention, tapping her cybernetic left hand on her console, watching the seemingly endless stream of incoming gibberish filtering through their ship's scanning array as the little craft performed yet another survey of yet another seemingly empty world.

"Hey, Cap. Anything interesting?" her first mate asked as he strolled onto the bridge.

"Not a damn thing, yet again," she replied. "And for the love of God, what the hell are you eating, Moose?"

Mustafa "Moose" Elsegy grinned and took another bite from his oversize cream-filled pastry. "Boston cream. The replicator finally got the texture right. You want a bite?"

"I have no idea how you can eat so much of that junk."

"Hey, my body is a temple, and I'm sacrificing donuts," he replied with a chuckle through his full mouth.

"Such manners," she said with a resigned sigh.

Captain Perez and her Number One had been a team for several years, ever since the survey missions after the Great War began in earnest, and the camaraderie––and ridiculous banter that often accompanies it––was well established by this point.

He was her right-hand man, and as that particular limb of his was a ceramisteel replacement running from his chest and shoulder all the way to the tips of his fingers, whatever his task, it was in good, strong hands. His right eye was less obvious, the cybernetic replacement designed to be indistinguishable from a regular old eye. But inside resided an advanced suite of specialized applications, though most hadn't found a use as of yet.

Their ship was a dumb ship. A non-AI-powered vessel. That meant the human crew was tasked with all of the boring, menial tasks the artificial minds of the larger ships in their exploration force would normally do. But they'd warped into a crowded solar system, and there were a lot of worlds to check out.

As a result, they'd been tasked with flying a grid over the cold world seven planets from the sun, while the others did similar runs around the other planets. This particular deployment was just another in a long string, and had already been underway a few months, but the hopping from system to system with their Chithiid comrades was still a welcome adventure for the duo.

Both loved space, and neither could imagine doing anything else with their lives. Not after seeing so much. After living the true life of space-faring scouts. They were the advance line, seeking out first contact, and it was a thrill.

The joint fleet of humans, their AI-driven vessels, and their alien allies hadn't had any success yet, but it was only a matter of time, they figured. After all, the Chithiid had wound up on Earth, and had become the planet's loyal allies. And after a good decade of cohabitation after the Great War that threw them together, seeing one of the four-armed, four-eyed, exceedingly tall aliens was just another daily occurrence.

The second set of eyes positioned toward the back of their head was still something of a novelty, though. It was tough to sneak up on a Chithiid unless you were directly behind them, and even then, the blind spot was minimal. But that didn't help them much when it came to space flight in larger ships. Their smaller, personal craft, however, did possess a unique canopy system to their cockpits that allowed for a far greater angle of sight than their human counterparts.

But on this mission, Sadira and Moose were on their own. At least, until they rejoined the others aboard their central hub ship.

"You wanna do another pass over the lower axis?" Mustafa asked.

"Nah. We've scanned the hell out of this rock, and there isn't so much as a trace of amino acid life, let alone something we can try to talk to."

"Ooh, chatty primordial ooze. I long for the day."

"You're ridiculous, you know that?"

"One of my many charms," he replied with a laugh. "Anyway, I'm thinking maybe we--"

A sudden flash off the ship's starboard side caught their attention. Mustafa's training kicked in, and he moved on instinct, powering up the little ship's shields as Sadira whipped them around to better observe the phenomenon.

It was a good thing he did, as no sooner had they repositioned themselves than they realized this was no solar event, but an actual alien ship dropping out of what appeared to be warp. And rather than a friendly greeting, they were met with a peppering of a variant of pulse fire.

"Going evasive!" Sadira said as she spun the ship away from the attack. "Moose, try to raise them on comms."

"On it," he replied. "Unknown craft, this is the Earth ship *Orwell*. We are on a peaceful mission and mean no harm. Please, cease fire."

The alien ship was unlike any Chithiid or Ra'az ship they'd ever seen. It was definitely what they'd been looking for. First contact with a new race. But this race seemed to want a fight.

Another volley of weapons' fire flew their way, and this time several pulses flew true. The *Orwell*'s shields handled it well enough, but things were getting serious. Their attacker was not only not responsive, but they were in a larger, and apparently better-armed ship. And they didn't want to talk.

"Sadi, we gonna shoot back, here?" Moose asked.

"We're trying to establish peaceful communications. If we can just find a way to--"

The *Orwell* shook from another direct hit.

"Oh, fuck this," Sadira growled. "Fire up the railgun."

"I thought you'd never ask," Moose replied, activating the ship's main defensive weapon.

"Can you target their drive system?"

"I'll be lucky to hit them at all," he replied as she spun into another defensive maneuver.

The larger, hostile ship seemed to have a different type of shield phasing, and while the few plasma rounds Captain Perez fired off from her console flew true, they were effectively absorbed by the enemy's defenses. The same could not be said for Mustafa's railgun, however.

A sabot pierced their shielding and tore into the craft, but the round went right through, coming out whole on the far side. The enemy ship quickly recovered, apparently sealing off the affected compartments and carrying on with their attack.

"Punched through, Moose. The railgun is turned up too hot."

"Copy that," he replied, quickly adjusting the weapon to fire at a lower power.

At supersonic speeds, if a round went too fast, there was a very real possibility of it simply poking a hole and exiting without causing damage inside. Slower, however, and it could cause massive damage as it fragmented and ripped through an enemy ship.

As if they'd only been toying with the *Orwell* up to this point, the attacking ship unleashed a far more powerful barrage, this time with what appeared to be their big guns. Sadira dove and evaded, but they were simply outclassed by the larger ship.

"We're in trouble, here," she said through clenched teeth.

"I know. Just hold on. I sent the pulsed distress."

"I don't know if we can avoid them long enough."

Abruptly punctuating her sentence, a series of blue flashes deposited several craft all around them. And those ships were not having any of this.

"The cavalry's here!" Mustafa hooted as their friends opened up on the enemy ship.

The pilot of the craft seemed to realize they were outnumbered, but rather than surrender, they fired even more aggressively.

"Why aren't they warping away?" Sadira wondered.

"I think I hit something important," Mustafa replied. "Look."

He zoomed in a frozen image of the rear of the enemy ship. A slow trickle of glowing power seemed to be escaping the craft where one of his railgun sabots had punched through.

"Shit. If we hit their warp drive, then they might--"

Sadira's words were cut off as the ship erupted in a ball of energy and fire, the oxygen within fueling the flames for an instant before the vacuum of space extinguished them for good. And just like that, the ship was no more.

"You guys okay?" Commander Jenkins asked over comms.

"Aye, Commander. We're intact."

"What the hell happened?" the commander asked.

"They just came out of nowhere and started firing on us. No attempt to communicate. Not a peep. And they wouldn't reply to hails," she replied.

A long silence hung over the airwaves.

"Nothing to be done for it, then," the commander said. "All ships, scour the area and recover whatever debris remains. We need to learn as much as we can about whoever they were."

CHAPTER TWO

The easy part of the recovery process was searching for survivors. With the scope and severity of the blast, no more than a few bits of flesh compressed into the few remaining ship fragments were all that remained of the mystery craft's crew. What was left of them was just tiny bits frozen in the cold of space.

As for the vessel itself, that had proven somewhat more robust than the flesh contents within, but it, too, had been reduced to no more than a scattered debris field of small fragments. It appeared that the explosion must have indeed hit the attacking ship's drive systems. What those consisted of, however, was anyone's guess.

A strange energy residue was still clinging to some of the remnants of the ship. Possibly parts of the power apparatus that drove the vessel. Or, at the very least, the remains of something that had been close enough to it to be coated with its unusual energy in the blast.

"Is that skin?" one of the human members of the retrieval team asked as they gathered up a gore-covered section of the ship's remains and bagged it for storage on the flight home.

"Indeed, it looks like it," the Chithiid handling the labeling and final crating of the recovered pieces said as his four arms worked at a fast, but careful pace.

"But, it's orangish."

"Perhaps a reaction from the blast," the alien replied. "Or, from exposure to the vacuum."

"Yeah. Or maybe they're actually orange," the human mused.

"The galaxy is an enormous place, with hundreds of millions of systems. It would seem reasonable that somewhere there might be such a race," the tall alien replied. "But, come, we need to get the rest of this packaged, crated, and safely stowed for the return to Earth. They will be most anxious to see what we've come across."

That was the best that could come from this incident. A new alliance had most certainly not been formed. Even so, all that could be retrieved were gathered up to be analyzed by the big brains back on Earth. Something good would come of this, though not what they'd hoped for.

Their mission, while a failure in regards to establishing productive relationships with new races––seeing as all of the newly found aliens were in tiny pieces––was nevertheless successful, in that first contact *had* been made. Just not as they'd intended, is all.

In any case, Cal and the other AI minds overseeing the data accumulated by the vast fleet of ships slowly fanning out from Earth in their quest would be *very* interested in what they had found. Obviously, this was a very advanced race. Advanced enough to possess some form of warp technology, as well as powerful weapons, as Sadira and Moose could most definitely attest to.

"Finally, contact. Only, it was the wrong kind," Moose lamented once the clean-up was complete.

"Yeah, and now we have to go all the way back to Earth before we even finish this deployment," his captain replied. "At least we're not too crazy far out. Just a few relatively long warps should get us back in the Comfort Zone."

The Comfort Zone was the part of space that the human and Chithiid teams had already explored. The stars were mapped out from their combined observations and provided a solid means of navigation for the AIs guiding each mission. Without those maps in hand, far longer warps could be made as the route was clear. Otherwise, who knew where they might wind up?

"Okay, looks like they're sending the go code," Sadira said. "Let's fire up the warp drive and go home."

The debris and remains were transferred to the main research facility located in the desert to the east of Los Angeles, the city where Cal, the massively powerful defacto leader of Earth's AI network, resided. The greatest minds in the system often congregated at his advanced desert workspace and hangar system, developing new technology and researching natural phenomenon reported by their scouting teams.

But now they finally had something to really sink their teeth into. Actual alien contact, though there would be no exchange of ideas or developing of a translation protocol for streamlined diplomacy, given the state of the creatures they'd contacted.

"No more than fragments of flesh," Cal said. *"What a pity."*

"Yeah, kinda hard to interrogate a meatball," Daisy said with a laugh.

Daisy was one of the heads of global defense after her role in the Great War. The survey mission she'd been out on with her bleeding-edge AI stealth ship, Freya, for the past several months had just returned to Earth a few days prior.

"You know we don't do interrogations, Daisy," Cal replied.

"Oh, just giving you shit, Cal."

"Yes, as you are wont to do," the AI said, amused by her snark, which was pretty much one of her main defining traits.

"So, what's the plan, then, Cal? You have any ideas?"

"Yes, actually," the AI replied. *"This alien species came from somewhere, and if they possess warp technology, it could be quite a distance from here. I'm thinking we need a truly long-range scouting mission. For far longer than what our current survey teams are performing, though. And much, much farther out as well. To the very edge of mapped space within our galaxy, in fact."*

"Sounds pretty cool," Daisy said. "How long we talkin' here?"

"Five years."

"Whoa. That *is* a long time. You know I'd volunteer, but my kid's barely a teenager, and—"

"I wouldn't ask you to go, Daisy. And I already have a few volunteers. Those who first encountered this hostile new race, in fact."

"Oh?"

"Captain Perez and Mustafa have expressed interest."

"Sadi and Moose? Oh, I love those guys. It'll suck not having them around for so long, but yeah, they're more than up for the gig."

"But we'll need something far more substantial than their usual craft for a mission of this length. And a larger contingent of crew as well. And they'll need to be volunteers, of course."

"Well, then. I guess, let's see who's feeling like a long trip to the vast unknown."

CHAPTER THREE

The massive AI brains overseeing the rebuilding of Earth after the Great War had pooled their resources together in the analysis of the remnants of the destroyed ship. With the sheer computing power they possessed individually now combined and compounded, it was relatively quick work making some sense of what they'd found.

A meeting of the leaders of the human, Chithiid, and AI contingents was called, and Cal's main facilities in Los Angeles had been selected to host them all. For the AIs, they didn't have to actually be present for the meeting, as their robust network allowed the sharing of information in nanoseconds.

The humans and their alien friends, however, preferred talking face-to-face, though that could be unsettling if you weren't used to the four-armed, four-eyed, inhabitants.

The Chithiid had lived on Earth for some time, and after siding with the humans and their AI partners in the Great War, a good many of them continued to call the planet home, blending into society and becoming a normal part of daily life.

Still, while four arms was easy enough to get past, the extra set of eyes toward the back of their heads tended to startle those from more remote locations who hadn't yet encountered them in person. A few who had fought side by side with the Chithiid, however, had, on more than one occasion, made a jokingly envious comment how that little genetic trait would help in raising their kids.

All present at the confab in Cal's spacious amphitheater space, typically used for lighter-spirited gatherings and presentations, were the best of the best. A group who had risen to ranks of authority during and after the Great War by their actions. Every last one was qualified for what Cal and the others had in mind. The question remained, who else would volunteer?

"Thank you all for joining us," Cal said by way of greeting, the auditorium's chatter silencing in deference to the powerful AI. *"As you all have been briefed, there was an incident only a few days ago. A first contact with a new race. And as you also know, these people were not friendly."*

A murmur rippled through the crowd.

"Now, we have analyzed the remains of the craft and have confirmed from traces of DNA recovered from the salvage that these aliens were definitely not of any species we've already encountered. Having spoken with our allies, we were already quite confident in assuming this fact, but now the analysis confirms it. We have also managed to isolate the unusual residue found on the ship's wreckage. It appears to indicate a form of warp technology, though quite different from our own. Zed, would you, please?"

"Of course," the AI powering the massive command ship in orbit chimed in. "What we've found seems to confirm our belief that a shot managed to penetrate the enemy's defensive shielding, as well as their reinforced hull in the drive area of their ship. The result was a catastrophic failure of the entire system, caused by a cascading warp power overload."

"What does this mean, Zed? Are we being invaded?" one of the human captains in the auditorium asked.

"Based on the reviews of video footage recorded during the incident, it appears this particular ship was not terribly well armed. In fact, it seems to be more of a long-range survey and reconnaissance craft, from what we can tell."

"They were looking for us?"

"It really seems unlikely they had any idea they would encounter our people. And this contact was far, far away from this, or any of our allied systems. But that doesn't mean we're in the clear, necessarily. Our tests seem to indicate a fairly robust warp potential within their tech, and as such, they could very possibly have been doing ultra-long-range reconnaissance. This ship could have come from very, very far away."

The captain seemed more than a little concerned. "So a threat from farther out than we've faced before? How are we supposed to handle a new enemy that could be from anywhere?"

"We actually have a rough idea of their originating direction, based on the faintest traces of that warp residue," Zed said. "It took a lot of sniffing, but some particles still existed. Enough for us to detect, once we knew what we were looking for. Tie that in with the video images we had of the craft's arrival, and we were able to figure out where it came from. More or less, that is."

"And that helps us how, exactly?"

"Cal, you wanna get to the good part?" Zed asked.

"Of course. As you all know, Earth and its allies are already running long-range survey missions of our own. Almost all of you have participated in quite a few of these scouting runs of your own, in fact. Far more than the others in the fleet. But with this new threat, the heads of the united fleets have come to a decision. We need to go deeper. Fly much farther than ever before, and by that, I mean far enough to warrant use of stasis pods for portions of the flight."

"But our warps cover enormous distances," a Chithiid captain named Hellatz noted. "This would mean——"

"Yes. It would be far beyond the comfort of an easy return home," Cal replied. *"And this new mission would be the first of its kind. A five-year voyage to seek out new life and new civilizations. For obvious reasons, it would be crewed on a volunteer-only basis. Thus far, Captain Perez and her first mate are on board. We are looking for two more to join them."*

A murmur again passed through the assembled space adventurers. A few months at a time was one thing, but *years*? And in deep, deep space far beyond contact of anyone you knew, human, AI, or otherwise?

Those with no family would be the obvious choice, but even then, most were not made of the stuff a mission of this nature would require. Fortunately, Sadira and Moose had already volunteered. They were well known and well liked, and the hope was that their presence would pave the way for others to step up to the plate.

"Five years?" Hellatz said, crossing two of his four arms. "And the opportunity to be the first ever to venture into these territories? My family was split up in the Great War, and I am the last of my line. It would be an honor to pilot a mission this important and have the song of my ancestors forever tied to such glory."

"Pilot it?" Moose said. "Cap's already got dibs on that, my man."

"Oh?" Hellatz said.

"Yeah. She's the best pilot in the fleet."

"Moose, please," Sadira said.

"No, Cap, it's true."

"Then let us test our mettle to decide who will have the honor of piloting this mission," Hellatz said with a grin.

Sadira couldn't help but meet his smile with a growing one of her own. Ultimately, she was going to be in charge of this mission, but that didn't mean she couldn't have a little bit of fun in the meantime.

"A head-to-head trial flight?" she asked with a merrily arched eyebrow. "Oh, Hel. It is *on*."

"Excellent. The crew is filling out. We will inquire for a science officer to join the team. And in the meantime, while you have your face-off, we will get to work modifying the ship you'll be flying for the mission."

"Yeah, it's going to need some heavier and more specialized armament," Zed added. "And ramped-up shielding. And, of course, the most powerful warp drive we can fit it with."

"You already have a ship in mind?" Sadira asked.

"Yes. One of our cleverest AI minds from the early days of the war has volunteered to be installed in this specially modified craft. He'll be receiving a substantial hardware upgrade for the mission and will serve as your pilot when in stasis, as well as an overall backup, overseeing the ship's systems."

CHAPTER FOUR

Getting to know a new crew was always a little bit bumpy at the beginning. Personalities occasionally rubbed the wrong way, and what one might consider benign quirks could drive another utterly batty. Fortunately, when it came to the new ship, at least, there was one constant they could count on.

Holly was his name. A top-tier AI from the early days of the Great War who had taken up the far more relaxing task of assisting Zed and the other military AIs problem solve the occasionally glitchy new toys their expansive minds would come up with.

It beat the hell out of fighting alien invaders for the very survival of humanity, that was for sure, and he'd already had plenty of experience with that. But with a new potential threat there was more than just survival and retaliation involved in this new mission.

This was an *exploration* flight above all else, and the likelihood of their actually encountering these hostiles––or anyone, out in the vast galaxy, for that matter––was rather slim.

The tantalizing thought of boldly going where no one had gone before was enough to tempt the more or less retired AI away from the cozy relaxation of his research and design activities. Sure, his AI core was an older model, but still self-contained within a large, sturdy cube, capable of being moved from one docking array to another, allowing AIs to switch "bodies" when needed.

Of course, most chose to keep the ones they already possessed, but a select few would occasionally swap to a newer model ship or a new facility within a city. In Holly's case, he would be upgrading to a bleeding-edge craft with far more processing power than his current system possessed.

It would take some getting used to, the additional mind space, but once he'd settled in, he would be able to expand and settle into his new digs at his leisure, as they traveled the vast distances into the unknown.

The rest of the crew would likely require a bit of a getting-to-know-you phase, though Sadira and Moose were well acquainted with their Chithiid pilot. Hellatz had proven himself to be quite skilled on more than one occasion, and he bore a confidence that bordered on cockiness—something of an anomaly among his race.

Goonara was more fitting to the composed and proper norm one expected of the Chithiid. She was also something of a brain, even among the scientific teams working with Zed and his teams. She found her work more interesting than people fairly often, and as a result, she lacked a bit of the social skills most found to be second nature.

That was fine, of course. Her duties were more fulfilling than any interpersonal relationships ever would be. She had met Hellatz in the past, but only briefly. So far as she could tell, he was a bit of a loose cannon by Chithiid standards.

"Are you prepared to receive a whooping of ass heretofore unseen?" Hellatz transmitted over the open comms line to Sadira.

"Oh, there'll be an ass whooping, all right," she replied with a confident chuckle from the cockpit of the little ship she would be piloting in this competition.

Hellatz had brought his own ride—a small, yet fairly maneuverable Chithiid transport ship that had been modified to his personal tastes over several years' time. It could carry a dozen people if needed, and would easily fit in Holly's new ship's landing bay.

It would, in fact, be one of two away ships stored there for planetary surveys, the other being an AI craft who had worked closely with Zed on several particularly risky missions. Ace was his name, and he had something of a reputation among the AIs, as any anomalous mind was bound to have. But it was precisely that different way of seeing things that made him such a valued asset, and Sadira was looking forward to meeting him.

For now, however, she had to focus. This wasn't just another simulation. This was a challenge to her piloting supremacy. The course they'd run was determined by Zed and Cal, spanning from the surface of Earth, out to a loop around the moon, and finally arriving back at the Schwarzenegger Space Port in Los Angeles.

A series of satellite markers delineated the path they would be taking, as well as simulated obstacles and enemies they would have to evade or engage as they made their way around the circuit. The whole process would be monitored real-time from Earth, the moon, and aboard Zed's command ship simultaneously.

"Are you both prepared?" Cal asked as the two pilots powered up all systems aboard their craft.

"I am," Hellatz replied.

"Good to go," Sadira added.

"Very well. Prepare to launch."

The two pilots readied themselves. It would be a hard burn, with weapons hot the whole run. The attacking ships would be simulated, and their weapons were de-energized and set to safe mode, so all firing would be of the non-lethal variety, given their proximity to friendly forces.

Of course, both were skilled pilots and would likely not damage their own allies, but friendly fire accidents did happen from time to time, especially in the chaotic, no-up-or-down battlefield of space, so all possible precautions were taken.

"Go!" Sid abruptly said.

Both pilots gunned their ships, the AI's sneaky starting command not taking them by surprise for more than a split second. The two streaked up into the sky, their onboard navigational systems plotting the general course to the next marker.

"Come on," Sadira urged her ship as she noted the Chithiid's craft edging ahead of her.

It seemed his ship was marginally better equipped for atmospheric flight, and as a result, he was slowly opening a lead. It wasn't much, and Sadira's sharp eyes and sharper reflexes helped her close the gap as she spun her ship into a roll, banking hard around the next marker.

It wasn't enough to catch up, but every turn let her more maneuverable craft chip away at Hellatz's lead.

"She's cutting it awfully close," Sid, the AI running Dark Side base on the moon, noted.

"Yeah, but Sadi's got the skill for it," Zed replied. "One of our best human pilots. If not *the* best."

"Don't underestimate Hellatz," Sid replied. "I've seen him fly."

"Hey, don't forget, I have too. Anyway, this is just the obstacle portion. Wait until they hit the zero-g combat element. *Then* it'll get really interesting."

Less than a minute later, the two ships burned hard out of the atmosphere, each pilot pushing their craft to its limits. The buffeting abruptly ceased as they both popped into the vacuum of space, immediately adjusting their paths and tactics to account for the different stresses of space.

"I see you are still admiring the *rear* of my ship," Hellatz teased.

"Just committing it to memory," Sadira replied. "Because this'll be the last time I see it."

She gunned her throttle around the glowing obstacles on her display readout, spiraling around the Chithiid's more linear path to cut him off at the next marker point.

"Oh, it shall not be *that* easy," the alien said, then abruptly changed his flight style into a matching spin to counter her maneuver.

Both were intent on taking the lead, which was precisely what Zed had counted on when designing this particular segment of the course. They would be focused on that task, and only the best of pilots would even register the swarm of hostile ships engaging them until it was too late.

Sadira saw them a split second before Hellatz.

"Enemy! Break right!" she called out, triggering her cannons.

Without missing a beat, the Chithiid reacted, matching her evasive maneuver just as a stream of simulated projectiles flashed through the space where he'd just been. He fired off a volley of simulated return fire, striking two of the digital craft. The distraction, however, had allowed Sadira to pull ahead, and she was now slingshotting around the moon, a full two seconds ahead of him.

"It shall not be so easy," Hellatz said, pushing his ship as close to the moon's limited gravity as was safe. Perhaps a little closer, even. The resulting slingshot launched him just slightly ahead of Sadira, but only by half a ship's length as the two raced toward re-entry.

"An impressively close race," Sid noted.

"We're lucky to have these two volunteer," Zed agreed. "We'll miss 'em here, but damn if this mission's not going to be in good hands, whoever winds up piloting."

The orange-hot dots high in the sky were clearly visible from Los Angeles as the two craft raced down at supersonic speeds. If the bright glow didn't catch the eye of those on the ground, the dual sonic booms certainly would.

Unlikely as it was, the two were neck and neck as they raced toward the hard-deck just above the sprawling spaceport in LA. It was anyone's race, and with drive systems pushing hard along with gravity's pull, it was too close to call. But Hellatz's ship was minimally faster in atmosphere, and at the last second, he pulled his nose a few meters ahead just as they passed the electronic marker.

Both ships broke away, scrubbing their velocity in a series of banks before landing in the spaceport. Sadira and Hellatz jumped from their ships and walked to the air-conditioned comfort of the facility's nearby buildings.

"An impressive show. Both of you," Cal said.

"Thanks, Cal," Sadira replied.

"Yes, your comment is appreciated," Hellatz replied.

"And we have a winner," the AI continued.

"Yes," Sadira said, turning to her Chithiid competitor. "Amazing flying, Hel. Really, that was inspired. Congratulations on the win. Looks like you'll be our pilot after all."

The Chithiid smiled and made a little bow. "Thank you, Captain. You proved to be a most admirable competitor."

"We'll be gearing up to go shortly. Why don't you get your ship stowed in Holly's hangar bay? I'll be along in a little bit."

"Of course. And, again, an honor to compete with you, Captain," the Chithiid said, then strolled out of the facility victorious.

"You interrupted me," Cal said when the Chithiid pilot was gone. *"You were the winner. Hellatz would have been either*

disabled or irretrievably delayed had you not alerted him to the enemy presence during the space segment of your contest."

Captain Sadira Perez smiled calmly. "All that matters is that *I* know. And Hellatz is part of my crew, and he's a fantastic pilot. I just wanted to try him out first-hand. A little dick-measuring contest."

"Though you lack the genetic prerequisite for such a thing," Cal added.

Sadira snorted, amused. "Thanks for noticing, Cal. And besides, a ship's captain lets their pilot do the flying, anyway. Regardless of their endowment."

Cal let out a low chuckle. *"Of course, Captain. Well said."*

"And we all know Holly is going to be doing all of the daily flight drudgery while we sleep during the longer warps, anyway," she added, "so it's a moot point for the most part. Now, when do I get to meet this little AI ship joining us on this mission that I've heard so much about?"

"Soon, Captain. Zed will have him to you shortly."

"Great. Then, until then, if you need me, I'll be over with Holly running through checklists. And, Cal, thanks for letting Hellatz enjoy the win."

"Of course, Captain. Congratulations, and good luck"

CHAPTER FIVE

Sadira walked the entirety of her new home's exterior, learning every curve and contour, as a captain should. This mission was her responsibility, and while Holly would keep a close eye on everything from an operational standpoint, she was nevertheless going to make damn sure her new baby was in tip-top condition.

She had made quick work getting her rather impressive ship outfitted to her liking. Naturally, there were a wide range of specialized additions made to Holly's new craft in preparation for the long-range expedition, but the captain had a few others she wanted to have in place. Things she and Moose had realized might be useful after their many missions together.

This would not be your run-of-the-mill scouting mission. In fact, it was unlike any from their world or the Chithiid's had ever undertaken. And with their strange attackers' warp drives seemingly capable of carrying the unidentified hostiles across vast distances, Sadira and her crew would be traveling so much farther from home than she expected humanity to explore in her lifetime.

"Moose, you talk to the supply master?" Sadira asked. "We're still waiting on that last load of gear."

Mustafa had just carried in the last of his personal additions to the mission's provisions. A specialized set of food replicator upgrades he would work on installing once they were underway. The ship possessed a small galley, should the crew desire to cook by hand, but it had been outfitted to feed them almost indefinitely with a fairly wide array of foods available from its replicator system.

But Moose had something of a sweet tooth, and more than a few of his favorites hadn't been included in the machinery's processing schematics. That simply would not do.

The device was meant to support and feed a military operation, but given the length of time they'd be away from home, a few creature comforts would hold far more value as time went on than the AIs who had outfitted the ship seemed to realize.

It was a simple upgrade, and one the AIs could have done for him, had he requested it of them sooner. But in all of the excitement of their new mission, it had almost slipped his notice. That is, until he asked the food system to make him a simple jelly donut.

"What the hell is that?" Captain Perez asked when she saw the solidified mass of red gunk slowly oozing from Moose's hands.

"It was supposed to be a jelly donut," he replied.

"Donut fail," Sadira said with a laugh.

"Big time. But that's okay. I got the parts I need to tweak the system from Habby and Cal."

"Your AI friends making sure you get your sugar fix?"

"Priorities," he said. "Any idea when the last of the gear is gonna get here? Hel and Goon should already have their stuff loaded and ready to go."

"I do wish you would stop calling me that," Goonara said, stepping from the ship. "And, from what I have been informed by Cal, the last of our supplies are due to arrive––ah, I believe that's them now."

Sure enough, a military gear hauler was rolling across the tarmac to their waiting ship, a stack of long and short crates strapped to its rear deck. The vehicle pulled up beside the craft and stopped at the cargo loading bay door.

"Hey there," the crew-cut man said as he jumped down from the rig and snapped a quick salute. "Corporal Dick Humphries, at your service. But you can just call me Hump."

"Hump?" Sadira asked.

"Sarge's doing. The nickname just kinda stuck once he plastered it on me. But I've grown pretty fond of it, truth be told," he said, unstrapping the cargo.

Moose knew they'd have a military support for security, just in case, but he hadn't met him until this very moment. From the captain's look, he could tell she hadn't either.

"Here, let me get that," Moose said, pulling one of the heavy containers from the vehicle with a grunt, his artificial arm easily lifting the substantial weight.

"Hey, thanks, man. I appreciate the help," Hump said as he effortlessly heaved a pair of the crates up and over each shoulder.

He clocked the amazed looks on Goonara and Mustafa's faces. Captain Perez, however, took it in stride.

"Corporal Humphries here is a cyborg, by the way," the captain noted. "One of Sergeant Franklin's spec-ops team, if I'm not mistaken."

"That you are not, ma'am," he replied with a grin. "They figured that with the rigors of this kind of mission, as well as the potential for things to get a bit sketchier than usual if we run into those nasty folks, it'd be a good idea to have me come along. That's fine by me, though. I've spent too long twiddling my thumbs, waiting for something interesting to happen."

"There was the Great War," Goonara reminded him.

"Yeah, but that was a dozen years ago. To be honest, I'm looking forward to a bit of adventure."

"Well, let's hope we have an uneventful flight, combat-wise," Sadira said. "Contact with new species? Sure. But I'd rather avoid knock-down fights if at all possible."

A loud boom rumbled above, punctuating her words as a little craft blasted into the atmosphere at high speed. The ship was sleek, and it was very maneuverable. It also appeared to be flying without a pilot. At least, without a flesh-and-blood one.

The AI craft buzzed the spaceport once, banking sharply into a corkscrew, then dropped down onto the tarmac just behind Holly's ship.

"Hi, everyone!" the ship chirped. "I'm Ace! I'll be coming with on this mission. It's going to be amazing!"

"Nice to meet you, Ace," Holly greeted her fellow AI. "It will be a pleasure having you aboard."

"Thanks. So, you want me to tuck in the landing bay, I assume? I would have gone straight in, but I saw everyone hanging around outside and thought it would be nice to say hi first."

"Much appreciated," Sadira said. "I'm Captain Sadira Perez. Welcome to the mission. Zed and Cal have told me a lot about you."

"All bad, I assume," the little ship joked.

"They say you're quite skilled," she replied. "Why don't you go get settled in. We'll be lifting off just as soon as the last of the gear is loaded."

"Roger, roger," Ace said, then blasted skyward in a flash, doing a loop before barreling right toward Holly's open landing bay door. He abruptly came to a near halt just before entering, dropping into a hover and easing inside.

"That one's gonna be a handful," Moose said, shaking his head with a chuckle.

"Tell me about it," Sadira replied. "But Zed felt he was the right one for the mission, and I don't question him on anything AI related."

"Probably a good call," Hump said as he pulled a small metal box from the loaded gear. "Here. Cal said you'd know what to do with this."

"What is it, Sadi?" Moose asked.

She opened the container, showing them the faintly glowing item held inside the small containment field within. "A fragment of the alien ship's warp-tinged debris," she said. "The AIs worked out a way to use it as kind of a compass. At least, they think they did."

"Yeah, Zed said this would work like an alien warp tech detector of a sort," Hump confirmed.

"Exactly. If we get close to an area that has had that specific kind of technology used in it, it should help guide us in the direction it is strongest," Sadira said. "Moose, stow this aboard the ship, load up the rest of the gear, and let's get ready to say our goodbyes to this gorgeous hunk of rock. We're not going to be seeing it for a pretty long time."

CHAPTER SIX

Hellatz sat in the pilot's seat, doing yet another systems check of the ship before their extended mission. He'd gotten to know the ins and outs of the ship well after he and his captain took a slow and detailed walk-through together. Both had the craft dialed in, and should something go wrong, both were ready to jump to work on whatever needed addressing should Holly be otherwise occupied.

Goonara was already in her lab space, merrily working away at her first series of experiments. An automated drip feed was set up for a fair selection of flora from both Earth and her native Taangaar. Being mostly vegetarian, due to the extremely high protein content of their native plant life, the Chithiid were especially interested in how multiple and extended warps might affect the germination and growth of the seeds they'd carry along to any new world they might colonize one day.

The humans had taken leave of the ship for one final handful of tasks, and then they'd be off. Not having an extended family to speak of, Sadira and Moose were rather quick making their rounds of farewells to their friends and neighbors. That done, they headed back to the ship that would be their home for the foreseeable future.

Five years in space was the longest for either of them by far, but utilizing the stasis pods on longer stretches meant they'd likely have more like four and a half years of actual up-time.

That was, of course, unless they actually encountered an advanced new race. Or, worse, if they managed to find the system of their strange attackers. In that case, they'd gather what intel they could and then make an immediate warp home, however long that straight shot back might be.

But space was a big place, and it was entirely possible they could go for months, or even all five years, without coming across another sentient and developed culture. The smaller surveys gradually expanding out from Earth had found some inhabitable worlds, but at most they contained animal life but no signs of civilization.

Holly had run several systems checks, though he had already dialed in every last component the moment his mind had been installed into the new ship. Cal and Zed had overseen the process themselves, and his good friend Freya had flown in to say her own farewell, as well as give him a little going-away present.

"I have something for you," she said. "It's a going-away present. Just a little something to tuck away, just in case."

"What is it?" Holly asked as Corporal Humphries carried the shielded container aboard and headed deep into his storage compartments to stow the present.

"It's a break-glass-in-case-of-emergency kind of thing," Freya replied. "You'll see. Hopefully you'll never need it, but if the going gets really tough, pop that bad boy open. You'll know what to do."

Freya was a very unusual AI. Her creation had been far outside of normal parameters, and her development was *different* from other AIs, to say the least. In addition, having grown up in a top-secret development facility, she was far more advanced than any other ship in the fleet, and by her own doing.

"How's the stealth shielding working?" she asked as Holly powered up his systems for the impending launch. "Dialed in?"

"Yeah. It's nothing like yours, of course, but it should provide at least a little buffer if we bump into any nasty types."

"Good. We want you to come back home in one piece. And how's Ace doing? I took him through his paces the other day when Zed told me he'd volunteered for the mission. Weird dude, but a solid ship."

"I agree on that point," Holly said. "But when it comes to weird, are you really one to talk?"

Freya laughed. "Okay, point taken."

"In any case, it should be nice having Ace and the Chithiid ship doing the surface landings. That will give me a little time to get readings from orbit while they deal with gathering surface data."

"Plus, they're not nearly as robust as you, and if shit goes wrong, you'll be the one keeping an eye on things from above," Freya noted.

It was true, Holly's ship had been outfitted with a fairly impressive weapons package. The railgun was stored in a retracted housing, to be deployed for emergency use only as it relied on sabots produced back on Earth. While the ship could fabricate more, it would be a huge drain on resources. For that reason, Holly would rely on pulse and plasma cannons instead, if need for firepower should arise.

But they all hoped that would never be a necessity.

"Is Hump good to go?" Freya asked.

"Yes. Corporal Humphries said just the other day that compared to the centuries he spent bored out of his mind when he was stuck under a mountain during the Great War, this will be a breeze."

"Yeah, Sergeant Franklin's guys had a pretty shitty go of it down there," Freya joked. "I mean, imagine being a highly specialized commando cyborg, only to wind up trapped away from all of the fighting."

"Until the end days of the war."

"Well, yeah. Obviously."

The crewcut soldier trotted out of the loading bay door.

"Okay, it's loaded and stowed, Holly. That's the last of 'em," Hump said. "Sounded like you guys were sharing war stories again."

"You and your spec-ops hearing," Freya said with a laugh. "We were just talking about the boredom under Cheyenne Mountain."

"Oh, don't get me started," the commando groaned. "Talk about boredom. At least *this* crew gets to sleep for the longer stretches of the flight. And the neuro-stim should keep their minds occupied nicely."

The neuro-stim device had been developed during the war, then perfected after, the technology adapted to function with Chithiid minds as well as human. The process was relatively simple. A slow trickle of knowledge would flow into the wearer's mind while they slept in stasis, gradually feeding them vital details of their mission, or new skill sets that would otherwise take ages of active study to learn.

But with a neuro-stim, the crew would learn while they slept. And once out of stasis, they would continue to gradually add on to their new knowledge, albeit at a slower rate. It was this technology that had allowed pretty much every human and Chithiid to speak one another's language fluently.

The younger minds of Earth––those born after the war–– were prohibited from using the device during their early years. The struggles of a growing mind were vital to forming a personality. But once they'd reached the appropriate age and had favorable test results, they would be allowed gradual access until they reached mental maturity, at which point they would have unrestricted neuro-stim privileges.

But this mission was comprised of older crew. Those who'd seen and done a lot in the war. And all had more than a little neuro-stim time under their belts.

"You'll be okay keeping firewatch while they sleep?" Freya asked, though she knew the answer.

"C'mon, Freya. Compared to all that time stuck in NORAD, these little stretches will pass faster than a fart in a convertible."

"Charming," Hellatz said as he exited the ship, safety goggles strapped to his face.

"All good, Hel?" Humphries asked.

"Yes. I was just grinding down a rough corner I noted on one of the containers in the cargo hold before coming to take in the sight of this lovely sky and enjoy one last breath of unrecycled air before we begin."

"Safety first, right, four-eyes?" Hump joked with a chuckle.

"You've made this joke before, yet I still fail to see the humor," the Chithiid replied. "I *do* possess four eyes."

"Ya know, sometimes, you're no fun at all, Hel," Hump grumbled, then headed back into the ship.

Hellatz waited a long moment, his face impassive, then snorted a little laugh when the cyborg was finally gone. "I do so enjoy pulling his chain, as you say."

Freya laughed. "Damn, Hel, a Chithiid with a sense of humor? This could be a long trip."

"And you're the one staying here," Holly said.

"Yeppers," Freya replied. "All righty, then. I guess this is it. You be safe out there, Holly. And come back with some cool stories."

"That's the plan," the AI replied as his friend lifted off and left him to his final pre-flight checks with his captain and her crew.

A half hour later, the crew was tucked away in their stasis

pods, ready for the first, long series of warps that would take them well beyond previously explored space.

"Sleep tight," Hump said as he sealed the last of the pods. The cyborg then walked to the command module and took a seat. "Okay, Holly. Away we go."

CHAPTER SEVEN

Captain Perez banged her head on the rising canopy of her stasis pod as it opened far slower than it normally would. That she had been abruptly woken and was still a little groggy didn't help the situation.

She rubbed her eyes and looked around. Something was not right. For starters, her eyes were a bit gummy. The stasis pods were supposed to keep that from happening. And why were things so dim? The lights weren't right.

A shape was moving quickly from pod to pod, she noted. Hers had apparently been the first to open.

"Hump? Is that you? What's going on?"

The cyborg turned his head slightly, his hands not slowing in their work for a moment as he manually pulled the releases and activated the emergency open sequence on Hellatz's pod.

"We have a problem, Captain," the normally jovial soldier said, all business.

"What kind of problem?" she asked, sliding from the pod and setting her slightly unsteady feet onto the deck. "And why are you waking Hellatz first? Get Moose up."

"Sorry, Captain, but we need a pilot more than anything right now."

"We have a pilot, Corporal. That's Holly's job while we sleep."

"Holly is down."

A hot flush of adrenaline surged into Sadira's veins. "What do you mean, down?" She looked around, her senses abruptly sharpened by the chemical rush. It *was* darker. The lights were dimmer by at least fifty percent, but the ship was making the subtle vibration it did only under one set of circumstances. "We're still in warp."

"Yes," Hump said as he moved to Moose's pod while Hellatz woke.

"How can power be out but we're still stuck in warp? That shouldn't be possible."

"Murphy paying us a visit," the soldier grumbled.

"Shit. But how is Holly out? He's a top-tier AI."

"Again, don't know, Captain. All I know is we're in a world of shit if we don't get this bucket under control. Ace is doing all he can, but he wasn't designed for this."

"Ace?"

"Yeah," Hump said, hurrying to Goonara's unit as Moose's pod began to open. "He's tapped into the life support and basic drive systems. Beyond that, he's way out of his depth."

"I heard that," Ace's voice said faintly over Holly's internal comms speakers.

"Don't split your focus," Humphries said.

"I know, I know," the AI grumbled, then clicked off the comms, devoting all of his attention to keeping the crew alive and the ship in one piece.

"Why are the lights dim? And what is the––?" Hellatz began to say. "Wait. We are in an unstable warp. Holly, what is the status of our drive and navigation systems?"

"Holly's down, Hel. I need you to get to command and see what you can do, ASAP," Sadira ordered.

"Immediately, Captain," the Chithiid said, bolting for the door.

He was more steady on his legs than she was, Sadira noted. Chithiid physiology seemed better adapted for the strains of this sort of thing. They were a hardy race, and that just might make all the difference today. Or not. She had no way of knowing.

"Cap? What's going on?" Moose asked, rubbing his eyes.

"Things are fucked, Moose. Holly's down, and we're stuck in warp. Hel's in command doing what he can, but I need you to shake off those cobwebs and get down into the guts of the warp drive system. Figure out what's keeping us in warp. If navs are truly out, we're flying blind."

"Shit. I'm on it," he replied, slamming into the side of his pod as his legs didn't quite do what he wanted them to.

"Careful, Moose. You're no good to me injured."

He nodded and kept moving, his legs steadying beneath him with every step.

"How long since we left, Hump?" Sadira asked as the cyborg finished freeing Goonara's pod lid and activating the open cycle.

"Just a few days," he said. "But the warp's all kinds of fucked up. No telling how bad."

"Right. We can figure the rest out later. Right now, we have to get this bucket out of warp."

"Copy that, Captain. But, how, exactly? I'm more the blow-shit-up-and-kick-ass department."

"We'll have to figure that out. And hopefully without any of our shit blowing up," Sadira replied. "I'm heading to command. Make sure Goonara gets up, then fill her in. She's a little one-track-mind when it comes to her experiments and whatnot, but we need her to put that aside and join Moose down below. It's not her specialty, but an extra set of eyes can't hurt."

"Two sets, to be exact," Hump said of the four-eyed alien.

"Hump."

"I know. Sorry. On it, Captain."

Sadira spun on her heel and made for the door. Her legs were much steadier now, and the wobbliness from the abrupt adrenaline surge had eased enough that her legs felt like her own again as she raced to command.

"Any luck?" she asked before the door had even finished cycling open.

"None," Hellatz said from his seat at the pilot's console. All four of his arms were working at a feverish pace as he tried desperately to find a way to guide the ship out of its uncontrolled warp without tearing them all to pieces.

"Ace, you still listening?" Sadira asked the air.

"Ears on," the little AI ship replied.

"What can you tell me about this from your AI perspective. Any idea what caused it?"

"None. I'm not a warp ship, so this is all new to me. I usually just fly. And there's no way to take any readings to line up with my onboard star charts as long as we're still in warp."

"Right. Well, listen, Ace, you're an AI, and your mind works at quantum speeds. I need you to peel off a tiny bit of that processing power and see if you can come up with any thoughts how to deactivate it. Just don't jeopardize your flying in the process."

"I'll try," the AI replied, then fell silent.

"Moose? You have any luck down there?" the captain asked over comms.

"Nothing. This warp core is acting incredibly weird. The lights are totally out down here. I had to activate one of the emergency backups to the backups. Something is making its power surge in a way I've never seen before. I'm worried that if we don't pull the plug, and soon, it may overload on us."

Sadira had seen what happened to the alien ship when they damaged its warp core. The thing had exploded in a ball of energy. They had only just begun their mission, and there was no way in hell she was going to let that be their fate.

"How long do you think, Moose?"

"There's no way to tell, Cap. But if I had to guess, I'm thinking we've got maybe twenty minutes before things go critical. But I can't be sure. It's all an educated guess."

"Thanks. Keep working. Goonara should be there any minute to help if she can," Sadira said, the few options available to them ping-ponging around in her head. None were good, a few were bad, but the only one she thought might have a chance of working was outright insane.

"Hellatz, what if we feed an energy surge to the drive dampers?" she asked. "Trip the emergency breakers and knock the whole thing offline."

The Chithiid was alarmed by the suggestion. "We would blow up, most likely," he replied. "And if we didn't, it would knock out life support and gravity."

"Which we could hot-wire to function if we bypassed other non-essential systems."

"True. And the power is too greatly reduced to be able to attempt that even if we wanted to. With the warp core pulling all energy to itself, we would need a substantial quantity to even hope to succeed, and we simply do not have that resource."

Sadira flopped into her chair, her brow furrowed in concentration. "There has to be a way. Hell, I'm almost tempted to go ahead and let Hump go ahead and blow—" she abruptly stopped mid-thought. "Wait, that's it!"

"Blowing up the ship is your solution?"

"No. Military stuff. The weapons systems."

Hellatz cocked his head in thought a moment. "A most unusual work-around. But those systems *are* backed up by a dedicated and separate power source, so they can still function in case of warp core damage."

"Exactly. And if we re-route that power into the dampers, it *should* throw the breaker."

"Knocking the drive offline and dropping us out of warp," Hellatz completed her thought. "It might kill us all, but from what Mustafa said, it sounds like we only have minutes anyway."

"Exactly. Nothing to lose," Sadira replied. "Okay, listen up, everyone. We're going to try something. If it works, we'll lose gravity and life support for a few minutes, so stay calm and conserve air until we get it back up and online."

"And if it fails?" Goonara's wavering voice asked.

"It'll be over so fast we won't even know it," Sadira replied. "But think positive."

"Yeah," Moose chimed in. "And if we blow up, at least we'll go out on a happy thought."

Sadira keyed in the sequence, her finger hovering over the execute button. "All right, everyone. Here goes nothing," she said, then jammed her finger down decisively. Then it all went black.

CHAPTER EIGHT

"Are we still alive?" Sadira wondered, as she floated weightless in the embrace of total darkness.

Hellatz's grunt from somewhere nearby made it clear that they indeed were. The telltale hum from their overcharged warp was finally gone. Unfortunately, so were the lights and artificial gravity generators. She just hoped the hot-wired life support system had stayed intact when they were whipped out of their runaway warp.

Sadira was so used to the false gravity on board that she'd forgotten to strap in to her seat in all of the excitement. Now, without it, she felt strangely at ease in the comfort of zero-g.

"Ow!" she blurted when the lights flickered, along with the gravity generators, their sudden activation dropping her to the deck with a hard thud.

"Are you all right, Captain?" Hellatz asked from his position comfortably strapped into his pilot's seat.

Sadira pushed herself up with a grumble. "Yeah, I'm fine," she said as more lights came on.

The command center's consoles began illuminating,

providing a tiny bit of information from at least a few readouts, though nothing like their usual data stream. The ship was intact. In fact, from what she could tell, there was no structural damage whatsoever.

They'd have to do a visual inspection of every last inch just as soon as they found a suitable planet to set down on, but for now at least, it seemed they wouldn't be venting into space. Of course, if Holly was online that would make the analysis a whole lot easier.

"Moose, Goonara, are you guys all right?" the captain asked over comms.

There was no reply.

"Mustafa, do you copy?" she asked again. "Shit, I think our internal comms might be down."

"No, Captain, they're reading as functional," Hellatz replied.

"Here, Cap," Moose's voice abruptly replied, accompanied by a medley of clanging and crashing noises.

"What was that?"

"We're fine," he replied. "Just some gear came loose when we dropped out of warp. Goon's helping me clean it up now."

"I do wish you would stop calling me that," the Chithiid scientist could be heard saying in the background.

Sadira allowed herself the slightest sigh of relief. They were in some pretty deep shit, but at least her crew was unharmed.

"Hump, you good?"

"Always," the cyborg replied. "It's been a while since I've been in zero-g. I almost forgot how different it feels."

"You're a machine. You don't forget anything," she replied.

"Just a figure of speech, Captain. I've been down here working with Ace to try to ascertain our whereabouts. It took a little jury rigging, but I got him hardwired into the ship's navigations array."

"And?"

"And I'm totally not designed for this," the overwhelmed AI

ship replied. "I mean, Holly's a Tier-One AI. He can handle this sort of thing no problem. But me? I was never meant to handle this sort of thing."

"We know, Ace. But this is an all-hands-on-deck moment, and I really need you to step up."

"I'm doing my best, Captain."

"That's all I can ask. As for the rest of you, do a quick survey for damage in your areas, then meet us up here in command." Sadira turned to her pilot. "How bad is it, Hel?"

The Chithiid's normally calm expression bore a hint of concern. For his façade to crack, they must be in real trouble.

"Multiple systems were overloaded when the energy pulse fed into the dampers, Captain. And, while you were correct in your assumption that we would not blow up, we are currently running without a sizable number of crucial systems."

"But life support is working. And we have gravity and lights."

"Yes. But from what I can see on the damage control system readout, the food replicators were knocked offline."

"Nothing we can't fix, though, right?"

"I cannot say for certain until we do a thorough assessment of the system. But in the meantime, I'm afraid we will need to rely on pre-packaged foodstores."

Sadira ran through the inventory of their ship in her mind. "I think we'll be good for a month at least. More if we go on reduced rations."

"Which is the wise course of action," Hellatz replied.

"Agreed. Once the replicators are back online we can replenish the supplies, but for now, it seems we're going to have to tighten our belts."

"I do not wear a belt, Captain. My uniform is tailored to my--"

"It's a figure of speech, Hel," Sadira said. "What I'm saying is, things could get uncomfortable. And Moose loves food, so he's going to be a miserable one until we can get it functional again.

Now, run me through the damage report on the drive system. I'm hoping we can at least limp to a relatively inhabitable world to set down and really see how screwed we are."

Twenty minutes had passed before Moose, Goonara, and Corporal Humphries joined the captain in command. Each brought the same story with them. Multiple systems were out, but life support and gravity held across the ship. Lighting was hit or miss, though, and there was no telling what else might be shorting out until they stopped for a stem-to-stern once over.

Worse, Holly was still offline and nowhere to be found. His central AI cube was intact, and the meter-square block still had power to it. But for whatever reason, the massive mind overseeing the ship was nowhere to be found.

On top of that, Ace was having a hell of a time steering the ship.

"I don't have star charts beyond what was needed close to home," the little AI said.

"An oversight on Cal and the others' part," Goonara grumbled.

"Not really," Ace said. "I mean, I don't have a warp drive, so it's never been something I'd need. I may be a kick-ass pilot, but interstellar flight is simply not my thing."

"So, we're flying blind, is what you're saying? Great. Just great. Game over, man. Game over."

"Stow it, Moose. We'll make do," Sadira snapped. "Now, Hump, you're an AI, and a pretty specialized one at that. What do you make of Holly's disappearance?"

The crew-cut soldier ran his hand over his chin in thought for a moment, though as an AI who could process things in nanoseconds, it was more of an affectation done for the benefit of the flesh-and-blood people around him. He looked human, but that was only part of it. He had to *act* human as well if he wanted people to be comfortable around him.

"My guess is he was connecting with the expansion storage when things went wrong. His capacity had just been increased by a massive amount, so it seems likely he was taking the flight time to flesh out his new body and mind space more fully. When the warp did whatever it did, it must've cut him off, somehow."

"Do you think we can retrieve him?"

"I'm not sure, Captain. But I can try."

Hump spent the next hour rushing from compartment to compartment, triple-checking equipment and ensuring there was no physical damage to any of the systems. Once he'd done that, he returned to command.

"Okay, everything checks out, so far as I can tell. I'm going to do a cascading reboot from the newest memory systems to his original one. Hopefully, that will push his mind back into his original body in its entirety, and a quick cycling through should bring him back online."

"You're turning him off and on again?" Moose asked. "Shit, I could have come up with that."

"You're welcome to try, cowboy," Hump shot back. "You have any idea how a Tier-One AI mind is structured?"

"Well..."

"Yeah. Proving my point for me. Anyway, we've got crucial systems sequestered in case anything goes wrong. I can't guarantee it'll work, but it's our best bet. Your call, Captain."

Sadira looked at the faces of her crew. They'd volunteered for this mission, knowing full well it would be fraught with danger, but none had expected this sort of thing so soon. But there was nothing to do for it but move ahead decisively, because she always said, accidents are caused by three kinds of people—idiots, indecisive cowards, and assholes. And she was none of those things.

"All right, Hump. Do it."

The cyborg nodded once then entered the sequence into the console.

The ship didn't make a sound. Its lights didn't dim. Nothing happened to key them in to what was going on within the great mind of their slumbering AI. Then, finally, "We don't seem to be moving?" Holly's voice said, confused and a bit *off* somehow.

"There was an accident, Holly. You were knocked offline and the ship was stuck in warp. We had to manually overload the dampers to force the ship back into regular space."

"Oh, that was clever," the AI replied, still getting up to speed. "But what's this? I feel another presence."

"Sorry, that's just me," Ace chimed in. "Hump hardwired me to help fly the ship while you were out."

"Really? Again, clever idea," Holly said.

"Yeah, but there's a problem. I'm not designed for this sort of thing, and my star charts are limited to Earth and the surrounding region. We need you to tell us where we need to go to get back on track."

A long silence hung in the air.

"Uh, Holly? You heard him, right?" Sadira asked.

The silence continued a moment. "I did," the AI finally replied. "But it seems there is another problem."

"Oh?"

"Portions of my memory stores have been corrupted. I'm not sure if they're lost or merely fragmented. In any case, I will attempt to restore and recover it."

"But you have your star charts, right?" the captain asked, doing an admirable job of hiding her concern.

"Oh, yes. Those are fine," Holly replied.

"Thank God. So, where exactly are we, Holly?"

"Not where we're supposed to be," he replied.

"Care to be a little more specific?"

"I wish that I could, Captain, but I'm afraid we've warped

somewhere far beyond anything in my data stores and star charts."

A cold knot began forming in Sadira's stomach. "What are you saying, exactly?"

"That we are lost, Captain. We are lost in space."

CHAPTER NINE

"Holly? What happened?" Sadira asked her mega-genius AI ship.

"We appear to have been stuck in a prolonged warp, Captain."

"No shit, Holly," Moose blurted. "But what happened? We were all in stasis pods, and Hump says you just switched off right out of nowhere."

The AI was silent a moment. Cyborgs did it to appear more human, but Holly was the disembodied voice of a cutting-edge scout ship. An artificial mind capable of lightning-fast processing, and with no need for such pretenses. So when *he* paused to think, it was cause for concern.

"Holly?" Sadira asked again.

"It...I——" the AI began. "It seems our warp was short circuited by traces of a foreign warp technology melding with our own," he finally said. "It likely caused a feedback loop into my systems, which caused whatever happened."

"*Whatever* happened?" Moose repeated. "So, you don't know what happened?"

Another long pause.

"The scrambling of the warp energies caused our own system to react in an unpredictable manner, and from what I can tell, the power increased the power of our warp, while throwing us off course," the ship replied in a decidedly female voice.

Sadira and the others looked at one another.

"Holly?" Sadira said.

"Yes?" she replied.

"What just happened to you?"

"What do you mean?"

"Uh, you're a woman now."

"Yes. And?"

"But, you were male. For hundreds of years, even."

"Again, and?"

The crew looked at one another. Their ship had just undergone what one would think would be a massive and life-altering shift as if she were simply changing hats. It was more than a little disconcerting, given what they'd just gone through, but Holly seemed to be fine, for the most part, and they had other things to worry about at the moment.

"Okay. Well, you just keep checking systems, then," Sadira said. "We'll get down to storage and see what's up with that piece of alien tech. Hel, keep an eye on flight systems, will ya?"

"Of course, Captain," the Chithiid pilot replied, his voice level, but his eyes conveying that he understood her wishes.

Holly was functional, but they needed someone keeping watch over crucial systems until they figured out exactly how okay she was. That, and they had to find out exactly what damage the supposedly benign piece of alien wreckage had done. Sadira set off at a quick pace, striding down the corridor with purpose.

"Goonara, you're the science officer. See if you can detect any anomalies in any of the ship's other systems. There's no telling what might have been affected by that piece of tech."

"I will do so, Captain."

"Okay, let's get to the cargo hold and see what we can learn from that little alien warp residue detector Cal and the boys whipped up for us. Looks like it may have somehow caused all of this mess."

Hump shifted the small bag of tools slung over his shoulder. "Right behind you, Captain."

"Uh, Cap? Hang on a sec," Moose said.

"What is it?" she asked, noting his slightly abashed hesitation.

"Well, uh, we shouldn't go to the cargo hold."

"Why not, Moose?" Corporal Humphries asked.

The man shifted uneasily on his feet.

"Oh, Lord, what did you do, Mustafa?" the captain groaned.

"Well, I thought that since the warp detector might wind up being a pretty vital piece of equipment, it should go somewhere deeper in the ship, just in case we experienced any damage to the outer areas."

"So, it's not in the cargo hold?" Hump asked.

"No."

Captain Perez was not amused. "Where did you put it, Moose?"

"It's down in the auxiliary processing compartment."

"That's right next to Holly's expansion processors," Corporal Humphries noted.

"And the warp core," Sadira added.

"I'm sorry, Cap. I had no idea it would cause any problems. I was just trying to be proactive."

Sadira took a deep breath, then let it go. It really wasn't his fault. Sure, he should have stowed it where he'd originally been directed to, but he was skilled at his job, and over the years they had worked together, she'd learned he possessed a sharp mind. This was simply one of those things. It sucked, but there was absolutely no way he could have known there would be any sort of problem with the seemingly inactive piece of tech.

"All right. First order of business is getting that thing as far from our warp core as possible. Far end of the cargo bay. You got it?"

"On it, Captain," Moose replied. "And, Captain, I'm sorry."

"Not your fault, Moose. Murphy just decided to pay us a little visit, is all." She keyed on the internal ship's comms. "Ace, we're going to be relocating a bit of alien tech to the cargo bay. You going to be okay with that?"

"I'm still hardwired into the ship, so I've been overhearing a lot of what's going on. Yeah, I'll be fine. I'm not a warp ship, so it shouldn't affect me at all. And my AI core should be fine. I'm not nearly as expansive as Holly, so I should be safe."

"And if not?"

"Well, priorities," the little ship replied. "Do what you've gotta do. I'll let you know if I sense anything strange. But without that warp weirdness going on, I really think I'll be fine."

"Okay. Thanks, Ace," Sadira replied. "Moose, get on it. Corporal, you're with me."

Mustafa took off at a jog, leaving the captain and the cyborg behind.

"This way," Sadira said, leading the way.

A moment later, they arrived at her quarters. She closed the door behind them, then keyed in a security sequence into the console on the wall, shutting off all internal monitoring systems.

"We can speak freely now," she said. "So tell me, Corporal, what the hell's going on with Holly? Are we in jeopardy?"

The cyborg shook his head. "We're likely fine, Captain. I mean, at least so far as her core systems are concerned."

"But she just up and changed on us with no warning. And as a result of that alien tech, it seems."

"Yeah, but you have to remember, AIs pick a gender early on, mostly to make it easier for the humans they'll be interfacing with. It's the same mind in there, just a different identification."

"So you think she's okay?"

"In that regard, yeah. It's unusual, but not unheard of. But the reboot did reveal some new quirks in her systems. Stuff we'll have to be very careful figuring out. Some of her neural pathways have shifted during the incident, and with the new processing units coming online just as it happened, there's no telling if there are any issues that might arise later. So, I think we continue as usual, but with an eye toward caution."

Sadira took it all in and nodded. They were lost, their warp was non-functional, and their ship had just abruptly become a woman. It was almost enough to make her laugh at just how far from their plan they'd deviated, and right after launch, no less.

"Well," she said, "this mission is getting more and more interesting."

CHAPTER TEN

All hands had been hard at work for the better part of three days as the stranded crew tried to figure out which systems were safe to reactivate and which would need to wait until landfall to address. They had life support, and they had gravity, so those concerns were off the worry list, at least.

Food was still an issue, as the replicators were still offline. They had plenty to get them through for the near term, but eventually that system would have to be repaired, as would the ship's lighting. It was on, but sections were still dim. As a result, multiple access panels were kept open so they could re-route power feeds manually to sections Holly couldn't seem to control.

It was an imperfect system to say the least, but at least they weren't bursting into flames or voiding into space, so that was something. The internal comms were still glitchy, though, and the temperature controls of the shower system were inconsistent.

Bathing was still an option, but you'd have to have fast reflexes ready to shut off the water in the two seconds it would take to become either icy cold or scalding hot. As a result, the crew was a little ripe, opting to forego showering until it was absolutely needed.

The relocated alien warp detecting unit had been silent. Apparently, there was no trace of that unusual warp technology anywhere nearby, though they were currently drifting in the emptiness between solar systems. With their warp on the fritz, there was little they could do about it, though, and not for lack of trying.

Everyone was working long shifts, stretching their skills well beyond their usual duties and training. But that was why this group had been pulled together for this mission. They were more than just volunteers. Many had offered to come. But these were the cream of the crop in terms of flexible mindsets, and, given the current dilemma, it was clear why the AIs behind the final selection of applicants had chosen them.

Sadira and Hellatz had each taken their little away ships outside to do a visual survey of Holly's overall structural integrity and had found no visible damage. Ace had added in a rather thorough survey for microfractures in the ship's skin with his scanning array, but Holly had come through with a clean bill of health.

As for the rest of the powerful AI ship, however, that was another issue altogether.

"Holly, any progress on the star charts?" Captain Perez asked as she swapped out yet another burned-out circuit from the infrared scanner system's console.

"No. But I'll keep trying. For now, a lot of my memory is more than just corrupted. It's scattered between my interlinked systems," he replied, having shifted back to his original gender once again.

It was something he had done a few times in the days since his initial shift, and the crew, while initially surprised by it, now took his/her frequent changes in stride without much notice at all. Holly was still Holly, after all, and that was all that mattered.

"Where do we stand on the warp core?" she asked, clicking the panel back into place and reactivating the energy flow to the unit. A puff of smoke wafted out as the device shorted out yet again. "Shit," she hissed, powering it off and popping the cover again.

"The warp energy generation and distribution system is stabilizing, and I've been successful in re-routing most of the glitchy parts to more stable aspects of the distribution grid. But the drive system is another story altogether."

"Still can't make a proper warp?" Sadira asked with a frustrated sigh as she swapped out yet another pair of circuits.

"I'm sorry, Captain, but I simply cannot power it up to anything near capacity for some reason. The energy potential in the warp core is still there, but whatever happened during the incident seems to have restricted its flow."

"So no warps. Just great," she lamented.

"Oh, no, Captain. We can warp, only it will be more of a hop than a proper warp."

"Which doesn't do us much good."

"Perhaps, but we might be able to daisy chain those little warps until we find a planet with a suitable atmosphere to set down and affect proper repairs."

That was the pressing need. Until they could set down somewhere with a breathable atmosphere, they couldn't risk rebooting several key components that might be culprits in the ship's glitches. The problem was, those just happened to be tied in to the jury-rigged life support system, which everyone was under strict orders not to touch.

Essentially, what was keeping them alive was also preventing them from properly fixing the ship.

"All right," Sadira said. "Since there's no point even considering putting anyone into stasis, we'll keep working on what repairs we can on the fly until you get us somewhere we can land."

"I'll do my best, Captain," Holly said. "It's difficult without star charts, but I think I can steer us to the nearest system, even with our limitations."

"Excellent. Let's hope there's a habitable world there. It doesn't have to be perfect, it just has to be good enough."

"The perfect is the enemy of the good," Holly noted.

"You just make that up?"

"No, Captain. But I cannot pull up the data as to who first coined the phrase," the ship replied.

"No matter. The point holds true all the same. Thanks, Holly."

"Of course, Captain."

Sadira shifted her focus back to getting the system whose electronic guts were in her hands functional again. They'd need it when they finally encountered new worlds. She had already made the decision to continue with their initial mission duties despite the current situation. Just because they were flying in a compromised state did not mean they couldn't complete their task.

And besides, the odds of them actually encountering the dangerous alien foe so soon into their flight––and so drastically off course––was slim to none. All they needed was a safe harbor in which to carry out the remainder of their repairs.

"All right, Holly," Sadira said. "If you think you're ready, let's start making those warps."

CHAPTER ELEVEN

Two weeks.

Two long, tedious, boring weeks.

The non-mechanicals had almost started to lose count of how many of the little hop-warps Holly had executed in their search for a system with a habitable planet. After so long without a solid hit, Sadira found herself almost considering having the entire crew suit up in EVA rigs and just rebooting the damn system in space.

Of course, that couldn't be done, and she knew it. The possibility of the life support being forced to remain offline for any prolonged period pretty much nixed that option, even if she did eventually want to go with it despite the inconvenience. So, it seemed, a long, soul-crushing series of little hops it would be.

Holly, for his/her part, was functioning relatively well, considering the damage he was trying to undo. His mind was a complex tangle of enormous streams of data, but with just a few little shifts in their pathways, he could still be somewhat unpredictable. And some of those alterations seemed to be more than minor.

Fortunately, Ace and Corporal Humphries were able to help

the AI, picking up the slack when Holly would hit a processing snag. They were all thankful, those were becoming less frequent.

The corrupted systems housing their star maps, however, were looking more and more like they might be irretrievably scrambled. They weren't flying blind, but they were certainly impaired.

And then, finally, they exited yet another warp, but this time Holly said the words they'd all been waiting so anxiously to hear.

"Oh. It rather looks like I've found us a planet to set down on," she said, shifting to her feminine once more.

"Thank fucking God," Moose said with an enormous sigh of relief. "I swear, I was about to lose my mind with all of these little warps."

"That's been long gone, from what I can tell," Hump joked.

"Ha-ha. Very funny, tin man."

"Ceramisteel and flesh, actually," the soldier shot back with a chuckle. "Far sturdier than tin."

"You're ridiculous. Both of you. You know that?" Sadira said with a laugh. "Plot our course and take us in, Hel."

"Copy that, Captain."

Her mood had lightened by about ten tons with Holly's announcement, and an enormous sense of relief had begun replacing the lingering feeling of dread. They'd found a world, and while they might arrive to find it either a shithole or an Eden, at least they could finally fix the systems linked to life support.

It had felt like an endless, Sisyphean task, with every step forward seeming to lead back to square one, but after a dozen systems and even more inhospitable planets, they'd finally discovered a world in the Goldilocks Zone. Not too hot, not too cold, but just right.

Given the large body of water covering a sizable portion of

the globe, it was almost guaranteed to have not only a breathable atmosphere, but possibly even a pleasant one. And on top of that, it appeared to possess a lot of green plant life.

"Any signs of civilization?" Sadira asked.

"My heat scanners are still a little iffy, Captain, and I'm only reading small heat signatures of minor animal life. But my optical arrays are functioning perfectly, and there do not appear to be any structures of any sort on the landmasses in visual range," Holly said. "If you'd like to do a few quick orbital loops, I can make a more thorough assessment."

"Do it, Hel."

"Copy, Captain," the pilot said, taking the ship into a series of passes around the globe.

"Confirmed," Holly said when they'd completed the fifth pass. "No sign of artificially made structures. No signs of primitive civilizations, either."

"Air?" Sadira asked.

"I'll run the full microbe analysis once we hit atmosphere, but my orbital readings show a perfectly breathable mix of oxygen, nitrogen, and carbon dioxide."

"Thank you, Holly," the captain said. "All right, then. Take us in, Hellatz."

The Chithiid pilot took control, guiding the craft down through the exosphere at as gentle rate of descent as he could, just in case there was some hidden structural damage that hadn't revealed itself yet. With the heat and vibrations of the landing, any such issues would make themselves known very soon.

"Look at this place," Moose said as they dropped down through the high clouds over a particularly lush forested area. "It's gorgeous."

"It is," Sadira replied. "Anything down there, Holly?"

"Almost nothing. A few tiny heat signatures of local animals, but nothing of any significant size."

"It seems like a good area to survey for an idea as to how this ecosystem functions," Goonara said. "And I can take samples of local plant life to catalogue for our people back home. Even if there's no alien race here, this seems to be a good way station world for future expeditions."

She was right, of course. While their main mission was to seek out the strange alien race that had attacked Earth's forces, that didn't preclude them from carrying out the other part of their usual scouting runs. Namely, mapping and logging every habitable world possible. And this was right up that alley.

"You're right, Goonara," Sadira said. "Hel, find us somewhere open to land. Holly's too big to set down with all of these trees. We'll have Moose and Goonara take one of the away ships back there to run a survey. Hump, I want you to go with as well."

"We expecting trouble?"

"No, but better safe than sorry."

"Copy that, Captain," the cyborg said, then hurried off to gear up. Goonara followed close behind, eager to gather her survey supplies and explore a new world.

"Hel, you and I will power down and reboot once they've offloaded the away ship. No telling if the sequence will affect the bay doors, so let's be sure they're out first."

"A wise plan of action," her pilot replied.

"And, Moose, I want you to keep an eye on Goonara. She seems to get a bit of tunnel vision if something really interests her, and I don't want her wandering off a cliff or into a cave or something."

Moose chuckled. "Copy that, Cap. I'll make sure she comes back in one piece."

"I appreciate it," Sadira said. "Okay, we're all set. Hellatz, set us down and let's get this show on the road."

CHAPTER TWELVE

The clearing the Chithiid pilot finally selected to set down in was atop a small mesa overlooking a lush valley no more than fifty miles from where their science officer would be doing her survey. From that elevated position, the ship would be safe from possible obstructions, while also providing them with an expansive view of the new world.

They would be making repairs, but why not enjoy the sights while they were at it?

Holly had once again confirmed the lack of any heat signatures of any significant size as Goonara, Moose, and Hump loaded her sample collection gear into the little Chithiid ship parked outside of Holly along with Ace. Captain Perez had decided that the smaller AI ship would hang back and act as an AI assistant in the reboot process, just in case the sequence caused any unusual problems that Holly couldn't handle herself.

"You guys be careful out there," Sadira said as her team took to the air.

"You too, Cap," Moose replied over their comms. "Don't go blowing up our ship while we're gone."

"I'll do my best," she replied with a chuckle. "See you all soon."

Moose feathered the controls of the Chithiid vessel and eased it up into the air. He was a good pilot in his own right, but Chithiid ships were designed for the four-armed aliens, and as such, he could only fly it in the most rudimentary manner. Fortunately, the main controls only required two hands, the second set being used to operate the weapons and shielding arrays.

But this wasn't a combat run. It was just a simple scientific survey. And for that, Moose was more than capable.

"Oh, man, it feels good to get some fresh air and feel the sun on my face," Moose said when they stepped out of the ship. "Smell that. It's utterly unpolluted by any artificial contaminants."

"Not counting our own emissions," Hump noted.

"But this ship's drive system is ninety-nine percent clean, and the warp drive on Holly is even better."

"True."

"So, you see anything, now that we're on the ground?" Moose asked.

"Nah," the cyborg said, switching on his combat vision infrared scanning package. "A few little animals running about, but Holly was right. Nothing of any size out here."

"Well, then, I guess it's just us and the trees," Moose said with a happy grin. "Come on, Goon. Let's go get your samples."

"Yes, yes. I spotted a perfect area when we landed," she replied. "And must you continue to call me that?"

"Probably," he replied with a friendly laugh.

"He only does it because he cares," Hump added with a wry grin. "You guys be safe. I'll keep an eye on the ship. If you need me, just holler."

"Will do. Okay, *Goonara*, let's go."

With that, Moose and his Chithiid companion strode off

through the trees, careful not to tread on anything she might wish to collect a sample of.

"Look at these things," Moose marveled, staring at the thick trunks of the tall trees. "The bark looks almost armored. I've never seen anything like it."

"These are alien trees. I would think you hadn't," the scientist replied.

"Yeah, obviously," Moose said. "Still, it's pretty damn cool. Anywho, lead the way. And hopefully we'll find something tasty while we're at it."

"But the food replicator is functional once more."

"*Partially* functional. It makes the essentials, but none of the good stuff."

"Your sweets, you mean? Well, I will endeavor to note if anything with that flavor spectrum comes up in our survey. But do not raise your hopes. The odds of stumbling upon fruit on our very first landfall are slim."

Moose nodded. "I know. But a fella can hope, right? Hey, what was that?"

"What was what?"

"I thought I saw something. Little critter, no bigger than a large cat. And its fur was pink. Or, at least, it looked that way."

"Likely one of the heat signatures the AIs noted on the way in. We will endeavor to gather information on them once we've completed the botanical survey."

"What do you need me to do?"

Goonara handed him a set of vials and a packet of individually wrapped collection tongs. "Scrape any molds or mosses from the trees. One sample per container. And try not to repeat them if possible. And while you're at it, if you happen upon any of that animal's scat, collect a sample of that as well."

"Great. I'm an intergalactic poop scooper now," Moose grumbled. "Gee, thanks, Goon."

"Enjoy," she replied, allowing herself a pleased little smile as she went about her business.

Back at the ship, the reboot sequence was well underway, and, as the captain had feared, the life support systems were indeed knocked offline, and for far longer than anticipated, while Holly cycled her fragmented systems back on one by one.

"How's it looking, Ace?" she asked the little ship serving as a second set of eyes on the process.

"I think Holly's got it all under control," he replied. "There are still all sorts of glitches in there, though. But that stuff is way beyond my pay grade. The reboot seems to have cleared a lot of it up, though."

"It's a start, at least. So nothing we should be alarmed about?"

"Not that I can see."

"Finally, a little bit of good news," she said, then strolled over toward her pilot.

Hellatz was fiddling with the landing bay doors as other components switched on and off. It wasn't a vital system in the grand scheme of things, like life support was, but he placed a great priority in being able to fully cycle the doors so the away ships could pull free if the need arose. Captain Perez was wont to agree with him.

"How's it coming on your end, Hellatz?"

"There are still a few manual override pathways that are showing some disconcerting delays, but the bay doors are functional, overall, despite them."

"So, the ships can get out if they have to?"

"I believe so, yes. But hopefully Holly will regain his full faculties and we shall have no issues requiring a manual override."

"I hope you're right," Sadira said. "Ace has been double-checking as the ship's systems reboot, and he thinks a lot of the problems are resolving with the hard reset."

"Which has had our life support systems offline this entire time," the Chithiid added.

"Yeah. It's a good thing we did this on the ground. There's no way we could have risked it in space, even with our EVA suits. Now, if you've got the bay doors under control, how about you come help me give these life support systems a kick in the ass and get them back online?"

CHAPTER THIRTEEN

Goonara was utterly enthralled with her work. There were so many new species of plants and insects for her to study, she almost didn't know where to begin. But as she and Moose crept along, gathering samples as they went, she found her groove.

One particularly unusual bit of scat on the soil near a grove of the strange trees caught her eye, pulling her away from Moose's side. She wasn't sure what it was, but the traces seemed to indicate a much larger animal than any of their scans had picked up.

She crouched down, her forward eyes intently studying the confusing traces at her feet. Something was not right, but she couldn't figure out exactly what.

Not ten feet away, the thick-trunked tree did something unusual. It began silently shedding its dense, armored bark. The scales shifted in color as the enormous lizard creature that had been wrapped around the tree loosened its grip and focused its gaze on the unusual, warm-blooded creature crouched down so close.

This would be an easy meal, unlike the much smaller and faster native animals. The creature tensed its muscles, then leapt, its claws outstretched as it flew through the air. Only the second set of eyes on the back of the Chithiid's head saved her, alerting her and sending her diving aside.

The attacker was upon her in a flash, powerful jaws and claws snapping and grasping, trying to take a chunk out of her warm, delectable flesh. But the Chithiid were a strong species, even the less physical science-minded of the lot. And their four arms made them a particularly difficult opponent.

The lizard continued to struggle, confused by the additional limbs, but not giving up, its snapping, sharp teeth far too close for comfort.

"Mustafa! Help!" Goonara shouted.

Moose looked up, surprised she'd wandered so far without him noticing. Then he saw the large lizard creature attacking her. She had that one pretty much under control, but what worried him was two more of the beasts suddenly becoming visible as they peeled off from a nearby tree.

"We've got hostile contact at my location!" he transmitted as he raced to her side. "Some sort of lizard things hiding on the trees!"

The two new attackers had roused fully from their rest and were about to lunge at the pinned Chithiid when Moose, not having a better plan, simply tackled them both, wrapping each of their throats in his strong hands.

The creatures were somewhat smaller than the human, but both of his hands were occupied, while their claws were free to swipe and tear.

"Fuck you, you fucking fucks!" he growled, smacking their chomping faces together as they dug their claws into his forearms. "Not fucking happening!"

But despite his best efforts, Moose was quite aware that his strength wouldn't last forever. He was losing blood, and his increasing injuries were making his grip begin to waver. His left arm twitched under the strain, allowing the creature to drop even closer, its teeth no more than eight inches from his face.

"No you don't!" he grunted, redoubling his efforts to hold the beasts at bay.

But his arms were about to give out, and much to his horror, there was nothing he could do about it.

A shower of exploding trees filled the air with debris, then a pair of pulse blasts ripped the two creatures from his hands. Moose looked up to see Ace in a low hover, trees blasted to make a hole. Sadira had jumped to the ground, pulse pistols blazing. Apparently, his captain had heard the distress call, and the AI ship had hit the afterburners, getting her to his aid as quickly as physically possible.

"Goonara," he managed to say as his energy failed him.

"Hump's got her," she said as she slapped emergency compression dressings on both of his bleeding arms. "Just hold on."

He looked over at where Goonara had been to find the spec-ops cyborg had left his post at the ship and run to their assistance. They'd covered a fair amount of terrain in their survey, but even so, he reached them quickly. Moose realized he must have been moving at one hell of a clip to make it to them so fast. Then he passed out.

"Hump, I need you to help me get Moose aboard Ace."

"On it," the cyborg said, hoisting Goonara to her feet, then, as soon as she'd gained her balance, rushing to his downed comrade. He picked the man up with ease, throwing him over his shoulder. "Ace, drop down six more feet," he called to the ship, the hatch still open.

"I can come a bit lower if you--"

Hump jumped up into the ship as if it were nothing, despite the full weight of the unconscious man he was carrying.

"Oh yeah, spec ops fabrication," Ace said. "Forgot."

Corporal Humphries quickly strapped Moose into a seat and

jumped back to the ground. "Come on, Goonara, I'll help you up."

In short order he heaved the Chithiid, then their captain, back up into the open hatch.

"Come on, Hump."

"Negative, Captain. I've got to get the other ship, and Moose needs assistance immediately. Don't worry about me. I can handle these things," he said, picking up the carcass of the lizard beast whose neck he'd violently broken. "I'll meet you back at Holly."

With any other crewmember, Sadira would have ordered him to get aboard, but he was right. As a spec-ops cyborg, he was more than capable of handling the creatures on the way back to the other ship.

"Okay. We'll see you there," she said. "Punch it, Ace."

The little AI ship didn't need to be told twice. He spun on his axis and raced back to Holly and her waiting medical facilities. Hump looked around. More of the creatures were peeling off of the trees. It seemed they were the apex species on this world, and he'd just killed one of them.

"Catch me if you can, fuckers," he said with an icy grin, then took off running at a pace over the uneven terrain that only a cyborg of his specialized lineage could manage.

Meanwhile, Hellatz had prepped the ship for their arrival, and Holly had fired up her full medical suite. That, fortunately, was fully functional, and the med pods were open and waiting when they landed. Hellatz and Sadira carried Moose into the nearest pod, Goonara following close behind.

"You too, Goonara. Into the other pod."

"But, I'm only minorly––"

"No lip. Get your ass in the pod," Sadira ordered.

"Yes, Captain," the Chithiid replied, then slid into the other unit.

Both whirred into action, one surveying the minor injuries

of the alien scientist, the other assessing the more severe damage to the human crewmember.

"You got this, Holly?"

"Yes, Captain. They'll both be fine. I've already set the system to work rebuilding the damage both have sustained to their flesh components."

It was slightly strange phrasing, but Holly was functional, more or less, so that was all that mattered at the moment.

"Okay, get to it, then," Sadira said.

"Coming in hot, Captain," Ace announced over comms.

"On our way," Sadira replied. "Hellatz, with me."

The two rushed down to the landing bay to meet Corporal Humphries. He stepped out of the ship with a few more spatters of blood on him, but given its shade, it was clearly not his own. And in each hand, he carried the carcass of one of the lizard things.

"Thought you'd want these for study," he said. "Make sure they're not poisonous or anything."

"Thanks, Hump. Get 'em into the isolation containers in the lab. We'll get to them once we're safely in space."

"We're not sticking around down here?"

"Not a chance. Those things didn't show on our heat sensors, and there's no telling what else might be out there. Enough repairs have been made for now, and it's just not worth sticking around."

"Copy that," the cyborg said, looking at the blood on the deck. "I'll dump 'em in the lab, then give the ships a quick scrub down."

Sadira noticed the traces of her friend's injuries. She'd need a shower and clean uniform. They all would.

"Thanks, Hump. We'll debrief in an hour."

They all split off to finish their tasks, leaving the hangar bay relatively empty. The lights flickered slightly, then a bit more as a pinkish, cat-sized creature with large eyes and a stubby tail jumped down from the Chithiid ship it had taken refuge in when the hungry creatures had gone hunting.

It looked around at its strange, artificial surroundings with confusion. This wasn't the forest. This was something totally different.

The sounds of footsteps rang out. Panicked, the creature looked around desperately for a place to hide. Across the hangar it spied an open access panel and bolted for it. By the time Corporal Humphries had returned, it was safely hiding within the ship's walls.

CHAPTER FOURTEEN

Mustafa was sleeping soundly in his med pod when Sadira and Hellatz came to check on him. The machinery had done its job quickly and efficiently, healing up his hurt in just a few short hours. But the blood loss had drained him, in a non-vampiric way, leaving his body in need of some good old-fashioned rest before he'd be ready to get back to it.

Goonara, on the other hand, had only received minor scratches during her fight with the alien lizard thing. But even so, she too was locked in her pod for the time being. Unlike Moose, her nap was of her own choice. There was little else to do while she was contained in the device, so why not catch up on a little rest?

"It's going to be a day or two," Hellatz said as they walked back to command from the medical facilities. "Normally it would take longer, but with the two fresh samples taken from the beasts that caused the injuries––thanks to Corporal Humphries––Holly can at least shorten that time as he had direct access to a source of any potential contamination."

"And while he does, we continue our mission. Even if we're shorthanded for a few days, we need to get back on track."

"I agree," her pilot said, sliding into his seat as they entered command.

"All right, then. We triple-checked the warp system while we were on the surface, and it all seems to check out perfectly. Holly, are we good to go?"

"Yes, Captain," he said, having shifted back to his masculine side once more. "Now that the foreign warp contamination has been cleared from our systems and my guidance units have been brought back online, we should have no significant problems."

"And your star maps?"

"While my original charts are still fragmented and unreadable, I have spent a great deal of effort creating a new set based on our present location. They should help us build an entirely new set as we progress."

"So, while we still don't know the way home, at least we're not going to be getting *more* lost," Sadira said. "It's a small win, but I'll take it."

She sat down in her captain's seat and gave the systems' readouts one more once-over, ensuring everything was functioning more or less as intended.

"All right. It's time to shake out the cobwebs, fellas. Hellatz, prep for warp. Holly, warm up your systems and give us one more run-through."

"Done, Captain," the AI said, his familiar speed and efficiency apparently returning after the additional systems were taken offline and rebooted. "Warp drive is functioning at normal levels and is primed for warp."

Sadira took a deep breath and let it out with a little sigh of relief. Finally, her ship was working again. Things were back to normal, and they could maneuver once more.

"Okay. Warp us out of here," she directed.

The warp engaged, whipping the ship into warp, covering vast distances in a blink of an eye. Then the ship rumbled and went dark, falling out of warp.

"What happened, Holly?" Captain Perez called out. "You said everything was working."

"It was, Captain," the AI said as the lights flickered back on. "This wasn't anything to do with our previous issues. There was a massive power drain from all systems tied in to the warp drive. It forced us out of the warp bubble and off-track. I'm afraid I'll have to attempt to create a new star chart again."

"We're lost again?" Hellatz asked.

"Yes."

"Again?" Sadira said with an exasperated sigh. "And we just compiled a barely useful new one."

"Apologies, Captain, but I do not know what to tell you. This was something new. And I don't know the extent of the systems it may have compromised."

Sadira jumped to her feet. "Shit. Moose and Goonara."

Hellatz was right behind her as she raced to medical. Corporal Humphries was already there when they arrived.

"Just checked on 'em, Cap. They're okay. The medical systems weren't affected."

Safely locked away in their pods, Moose and Goon were banging on the glass, wide awake and wanting out.

"Open this thing up. We can help."

"Sorry, Moose, but you need to stay put for a bit longer," Sadira said.

"But the healing process is long finished."

"Mustafa is correct," Goonara said. "We are both more than ready to exit these healing pods."

"You know we can't do that," Humphries said. "Rules are rules. It was an alien attack. It's pathogen protocol. Quarantine."

"I'm sorry, Goonara, but he's right. You're our science officer and know better than most what the protocols are for direct contact with a possible alien pathogen," Sadira told her.

The Chithiid took a deep breath and calmed herself. "Of

course, Captain. But there has to be some way we can be of help, even while stuck in these vessels."

"Not that I can think of, so just sit tight and relax. Holly's working as fast as he can to process the alien carcasses and clear you two of any possible contagion exposure. Once that's been done, we'll get you out of there, I promise."

"For now, Captain, I suggest we make haste to the warp core to ascertain if there has been any physical damage incurred during this latest incident."

"You go, Hel. I'll be right behind you."

"Very well, Captain," the Chithiid said, then hurried off to the warp core.

"Moose, you're sure that alien warp thing is in the cargo hold, right?"

"One hundred percent, Cap. It's as far from the warp core as I could store it."

"Ace? Anything in the hangar?"

"Nothing, Captain. All quiet down here."

"Well, shit. Come on, Corporal, it looks like we've got another freakin' mystery to solve."

The captain and her cyborg crewman hustled out of the medical bay to begin the tedious process of tracking down whatever the hell this new problem might be.

Moose and Goonara had nothing more to do but sit in their pods, wanting to be of use, but stuck, helpless.

In a flash, a blur of pink fur darted out of the open access panel in the compartment and out of the open door into the corridor.

"Did you see that?" Moose exclaimed.

"See what?"

"That thing!"

"What thing, Mustafa? I didn't see anything."

Moose rubbed his eyes. "I know I saw something," he

replied, then began banging on the pod's lid. "Goddammit, get us out of here!"

CHAPTER FIFTEEN

"I'm telling you, I saw it," Moose said through the thick glass of his pod. "You've gotta believe me, Cap, there's a thing on board. Tell her, Goon."

"I saw no such thing," the Chithiid replied. "But his description of the creature he claims to have caught a glimpse of does align with one of the native animals I observed on that planet before we were attacked."

"Look at the access panel. That's where it came out of," Moose urged.

Sadira and Corporal Humphries shared a look, then walked to the panel to see if his claims had any merit. Interestingly enough, there actually seemed to be something there. Sadira bent down and plucked a single strand of what looked an awful lot like pink fur from the edge of the opening.

"You seeing this, Hump?"

"Yeah."

"That look like pink fur to you?"

"Yeah."

Sadira sighed. "Great. So now it looks like there's a good chance we've got a stowaway on the ship. Wonderful." She turned her attention to the ship itself. "Holly, I don't suppose you can track this thing, can you?"

"If you mean do I have the ability to trace the location of a non-crew entity, then no."

"I was afraid of that."

"*But*, if I switch to a heat signature analysis of internal aspects of the ship itself, I may be able to detect fluctuations in the standard temperature of each compartment. If there is a variance of more than a few tenths of a degree, then I may be able to pinpoint possible locations."

"So, do it," Sadira said. "Run the analysis."

"I already am, Captain. But I am currently not reading any temperature variances sufficient to indicate an alien life-form presence."

The lights flickered abruptly, then slowly powered back up.

"Uh, Holly?"

"Yes, I am aware."

"Aware of what, exactly?"

"That something is pulling power from different systems within the ship, and in a manner similar to the warp core drain that dropped us into our current predicament. And it is not occurring in my common spaces. This appears to be originating from within the Narrows."

Sadira groaned. "You're telling me we've got a creature that sucks power from our ship, and it's running amok in your walls?"

"Pretty much, yes," the AI replied as the lights flickered again. "And I fear that unless we control this situation, we will not only be unable to warp, but we may be at far greater risk from power loss to other systems as well."

"Cap, you've gotta let us out of here," Moose pleaded. "Come on, Holly. You've run the analysis on those dead lizard things. What are the odds we've been infected with some mystery contagion?"

"Approximately one-thirtieth of one percent," the AI replied.

"Sadi, look at me," Moose said, addressing her as not only his captain, but his friend. "This is a life-or-death situation here, and I think if ever there was a reason to ignore quarantine protocols, this is it."

The captain knew he was right. Hell, she'd wanted to let him out the second he was healed, but they had a protocol, and they had to abide by its rules. That is, until now.

"Fuck it. Let 'em out, Hump."

"You got it, Cap," the cyborg replied.

"Hel?" she called out over comms.

"Yes, Captain?"

"Bad news. It looks like we've got an alien stowaway that's causing these power issues. Keep your eyes out for any fluctuations, and let me know the system affected. Holly thinks it's in our walls somewhere."

"An alien creature stealing our power? How did this happen?"

"No idea, but if we don't kill it soon, there's no telling what systems it might compromise."

"I will be on alert and monitoring from my station. I will be sure to inform you if I see anything out of parameters."

"Good. Moose and Goonara are going to be running a search on the lower levels, while Corporal Humphries and I will survey the uppers."

"A suggestion," Holly interjected.

"Yes, Holly?"

"I was thinking. If this creature absorbs energy as a part of its natural physiology, perhaps we can also track it by minuscule decreases in system power levels as it moves."

"You're saying you think it takes our power even when it's not actively trying?"

"I do not know for sure, but it seems to be a reasonable

hypothesis, even one which pursuing parallel to our other investigations, would not hinder them in the slightest."

The power fluctuated again, and this time the gravity generators kicked off for a moment. It wasn't long, but it was long enough for all of the crew to nearly fall as they abruptly floated, then dropped back to the deck.

"Okay, this is getting serious. Do it, Holly. Anything and everything you can think of to track this thing down before it causes some real harm," Sadira said. "Ace, I want you to chip in. Take off and scan the hull from the outside and see if you find any anomalies."

"Copy that, Captain," the ship said, setting to work decompressing the hangar, then launching to perform his sweep of the ship.

Captain Perez was more than a little concerned. This new problem on top of the prior ones was just the icing on the shit cake they'd been served, and this was turning out to be one big slice. And it didn't even have candles.

Their warp system was once again not functional, and clearly not safe to use even if it was, for that matter. And, with their abrupt drop from their planned warp, their nascent star map reconstruction was a wash to boot, forcing them to start from scratch yet again.

It sucked, in no uncertain terms. Sadira had somehow found herself pretty much back to square one. At least they had food and stable life support after their repairs and reboot, so that was a plus, but with this deadly little creature tearing up their power feeds, even those small mercies could be snatched away in an instant.

They had to eliminate the threat, and immediately at that. That was all there was to it. Anything less and there was a very real possibility they might not live to see tomorrow. The question was, how could they track and kill something they neither knew nor understood?

CHAPTER SIXTEEN

"Ow! Fucker!" Sadira hissed, rubbing her head where it had banged on the low metal ceiling of the crawlspace she was slowly inching her way through. "Yep. It's definitely in the Narrows," she informed the others over comms.

"You sure?" Moose asked.

"Yeah, I'm sure. I just found a little present from that little turd," she said as she pulled a rag from her pocket to wipe the creature's droppings from her palm.

"Save it for study!" Goonara chimed in. "We can learn much of a species from scatological sampling."

Sadira folded the rag and tucked it into her pocket, consoling herself with the fact that at least it didn't smell bad. In fact, the little animal's poop didn't smell bad at all, all things considered. Of course, with a diet of energy, as well as whatever it ate, they were in pretty much uncharted waters, in terms of intergalactic fecal aromas.

"Anyone else having any luck?" Sadira asked as she placed a small cube of bait food against the wall before continuing on her way.

"Nothing here," Hump said from his section of the ship's crawlspaces.

"Nor I," Goonara added.

"Moose? You find anything?"

"Not yet, but I've got a feeling it may be nearby."

"Well, you be careful. There's no telling what this thing might be capable of."

"Copy that, Cap," he said, then continued on his hands-and-knees circuit of the tight spaces surrounding the warp core and its key systems.

They had already tried outright pursuit when it appeared the little creature had ventured out from the crawlspaces, but none had managed to see more than the briefest flash of pink fur as the surprisingly fast creature evaded them with ease. Even when they cornered it—or so they thought—they found the compartment Holly had tracked its minor heat signature into empty, the access panel to the Narrows pried free.

"Little bastard is strong," Hump noted as he inspected the panel. "We'll have to secure these things better if we hope to keep it from just running back into the walls."

"What were you thinking, Corporal?" Sadira asked.

"Nothing drastic. Just some high-test patching adhesive should do it. It's strong, but the thing simply lacks the leverage to pull that stuff free."

"Duct tape?" Moose asked. "We've got a space monster in our crawlspaces and you want to use duct tape?"

"A thousand and one uses, my friend. Now a thousand and two."

"All right, Hump, make it so," Sadira said. "Everyone else, meet at the galley. We're going to have the food replicator whip up something this thing might find tempting. We've got to lure that thing out of the walls, and fast. There's no telling what kind of damage it may cause if it feed on our ship's power systems again. Next time could be catastrophic."

They'd settled on a combination of mostly fruit and vegetable matter, with a separate, smaller cube of a meat-like substance. They simply didn't know if the thing was an herbivore, a carnivore, or an omnivore. But seeing as its home world didn't possess warp drives and power systems, they were pretty confident it had to eat something other than energy when it wasn't graced with so tempting a food source as their ship.

The team spread out, each taking a section of the spaces throughout the ship. Some were simply too small for any of them to maneuver in, but they hoped if the creature was hiding in one of them, the smell of food might lure it out.

Moose was assigned the area around the warp core, but before he crawled in, he pocketed a handful of small power cells. His thinking was, if the creature favored energy over regular food, maybe a power cell rigged to leak a bit might be a tempting treat.

He was midway through laying the long trail of food cubes and power cells toward the lone hatch he had left unsealed. All other accessways to the area around the warp core had been sealed up tight as a drum. If they got the thing out, it would not be getting back in. At least, not to that particular area.

A little scuffling sound caught Moose's attention. He froze, heart pounding, adrenaline spiking in his veins. The thing was nearby. And it sounded like it was coming toward him.

"Shit," he hissed, hurrying back toward the opening, leaving a trail of tempting treats behind him as he went.

The sound persisted, growing a little louder still. Small feet padding along the metal deck, the occasional *clack-clack* of claws sounding along the space as it grasped for purchase on the smooth surface.

Moose made it to the exit and spilled out into the safety and space of the ship's interior. At least out here he could run.

"It's in the walls by the warp core, Sadi," he quietly said over comms. "It seems to be coming toward me."

"Hang tight, Moose. We're coming to you," she replied.

He appreciated the support, but he also knew it would take the others time to get out of their sections of crawlspace. It was a very real possibility that this was on his shoulders alone. He grabbed the weapon he'd left waiting outside the access hatch and prepared himself for whatever hell this thing was. When it came out, he'd blast it into oblivion.

They couldn't use pulse pistols within the confines of the Narrows, especially not in proximity to any of the ship's sensitive systems, which was pretty much everywhere the Narrows wove through the walls. But now, freed of those constraints, he could light that little bastard up.

Moose switched off the safety and eased his back against the wall outside the opening. The sounds of crawling had slowed, replaced by a faint chewing. The lure was actually working. He leaned down and glanced inside the opening.

Far down the crawlspace was a small, pink creature with medium length pink fur, floppy ears that seemed ready to spring up in attention at any moment, and large, gray eyes. Moose felt his finger ease where it had been resting on the slide of the pulse pistol. The little critter didn't look all that dangerous. In fact, it looked almost cute.

The animal glanced up from its meal, ears popping up to attention as it locked eyes with Moose. It paused a long moment, then returned to eating, keeping one wary eye on the man at the end of the passageway.

"Doesn't matter if it's cute," Moose muttered, standing back up and moving to a position across the chamber where he could get a clean shot at it when it exited. "Got a job to do, and I'm gonna do it."

He then crouched down and waited. It shouldn't be long, he reasoned. The animal seemed quite hungry, given the speed at which it had been eating the food cubes. Apparently, energy was a food source, but it needed regular sustenance too. He was musing how the little animal's digestive system might actually function when a flash of pink streaked out of the open accessway and out into the corridor.

"Shit!"

The creature had bolted, but rather than pursue, he raced to the panel and sealed it tight. It was a choice. Chase the creature and possibly fail, or make damn sure it was at least locked out of the area near their warp systems. It was an easy decision.

He was applying the last strip of adhesive to the panel seam when Sadira and Hump came racing in.

"Where is it? Did you get it?" she asked.

"No, Cap, I couldn't get a shot off. Sorry. It was just too fast. But at least it's out of the section near the warp core, and it can't get back in."

Sadira sighed. She'd hoped to negate the threat entirely, but Moose was right. At least the warp system was safe from further compromise. With the creature no longer sucking power from their already-sketchy drive system, they could finally attempt a warp again. At least, she hoped so. But other systems were still at risk.

"How are power readings, Holly?" Sadira asked.

"Fluctuations seem to have stabilized, Captain," the ship replied.

"Good news, for once," she said. "Now we just have to find that thing before it messes up some other systems."

"Uh, Captain?" Ace chimed in. "I think it's in the hangar."

"You see it?"

"Well, no, but that alien warp detector thingy? Its power levels just took a big dip. Wait. It's returning to normal. False alarm, I think."

Goonara joined them in the compartment, winded from her rush from the crawlspace to examine the dead animal that was not dead, nor captured.

Sadira looked at the scientist. "You hear that?"

"Yes, Captain."

"That's not normal, right?"

"No, it is not."

"So, it's likely that thing somehow pulled energy from the alien warp as well as ours," she mused. "Fascinating. We've already seen that those are very incompatible forms of warp power, kind of like mixing water and oil, but this thing can take them both in without a problem."

"And in passing, it seems," Goonara added. "The device is safely stowed, so it looks as if proximity is all that it requires. But how close, we don't know."

"Well, shit," Sadira said with a sigh. "That means it can still pull from the ship's systems, most likely, and we have no idea how."

CHAPTER SEVENTEEN

The warp system was apparently not as solid as Sadira had hoped. Despite the unwanted guest no longer tapping into its power from close proximity, the drive still appeared to have some issue that would take some time to figure out.

Just as disconcerting was that Holly was finding herself cut off from a fairly large number of the ship's systems. It was as if they'd simply ceased to exist, though they obviously hadn't gone anywhere. Most disconcerting was the abrupt loss of pressure in one of the storage compartments just after Hellatz had stepped out. A minute earlier and he'd have suffocated.

"What the hell happened, Holly?" Sadira asked. "This is nowhere near the warp core, and we haven't seen any major power fluctuations in a few hours."

"I know, Captain. But even the minor power interruptions are proving problematic."

"Problematic? I think nearly spacing one of our crew is more than merely problematic," Moose interjected.

"Hellatz would not have been ejected into space, Mustafa. The compartment merely lost pressure, from what I've been able to ascertain."

"Obviously, but you get the gist," he shot back. "The point is, your systems are still having issues, and I don't think they're entirely due to the alien creature mucking up the works."

"On that, we agree," Holly said. "Despite my best efforts, my neural fragmentation appears to have left me with quite a number of blind spots in my systems."

"Blind as in, you can't even see them?" Moose asked the AI ship.

"Precisely. I know the pathways, and they should be there, but for whatever reason, I simply cannot see them anywhere on my internal framework."

Sadira weighed this information and was not pleased with the implications. For a massively powerful AI ship to not only be glitching, but to also have some of its systems acting autonomously, was not good. And they'd almost lost Hellatz to a freak decompression. Steps had to be taken, and there was only one person remotely capable of stepping up to the task. And he wouldn't be happy about it.

"You want me to do what?" Ace asked. "You do realize, this is so far outside of my parameters, it's in another time zone, right?"

"I do, Ace," Sadira replied. "But we need to back up as much of this sequestered data as possible, and if Holly can't even see it, we'll need you to do the heavy lifting. It's AI stuff, not normal computing, and you're the only other AI for light years in any direction."

"So far as you know."

"Yes, so far as I know," she replied. "Now, I need you to see if you can work with Holly to tie back into the ship and help stabilize the things that aren't showing up on her systems. I don't need you to fly the ship again. Just do whatever you can to ease the load."

"Okay, I'll do what I can," the little AI ship replied. "I won't be able to fly any away missions so long as I'm tied in, though. I'll need to have Hump hardline me directly into the ship again."

"Nothing wireless?" Moose asked.

"I can't. Not with that creature messing around with power flows. Too much of a chance of disconnecting in the middle of something important."

"I'll be right down," Corporal Humphries said. "Captain, unless you need me for something, I'll get right on that."

"Go, Corporal. Get him tied in, then get your ass back to help us track this pest down."

"Copy that," the cyborg said, taking off at a quick-time jog to the hangar.

Sadira looked at the remaining crewmembers. They'd all been working hard since their initial warp problem, but there was no letting up on the gas pedal now.

"All right. Moose, you said you got a good look at this thing when it was eating."

"Yeah, Cap. Kinda cute, actually. It seemed to be really hungry, like the power it's been stealing isn't its food of choice. Obviously, we have no way of knowing how it works, but my guess is, we can probably keep it from entering more sensitive areas of the ship by leaving out small amounts of food for it."

"Like sacrificial snacks for the ants," Sadira joked.

"Sacrificial *what*?" Hellatz asked, confused.

"It's an old Earth picnic thing. You leave out something tempting as a gimme for the ants so they'll leave your picnic alone."

"And this actually works?"

"Well, no, not really. But it's a fun theory, and in this case, it just might work."

"We should offer up some power cells too," Moose suggested. "In case it wants to vary its diet. Might as well give it some easy power that doesn't make the ship go dark."

"Good call. Pull whatever rechargeable power cells we can spare and hand them out. We'll use them as part of the process."

• • •

They had produced a reasonable quantity of food cubes for the little alien beast, and after a few days, they'd managed to keep it contained within a relatively small section of the ship, having directed it there by slowly shifting and eventually removing feeding stations, essentially herding it there.

They also noted the power cells were being drained. Not regularly, but every so often. And more importantly, along with that was the far less frequent power drains on other ship's systems. It seemed the plan was working.

Mustafa even saw the little animal more frequently as it fed. It wouldn't let him come anywhere near, and any sudden movement such as drawing a pulse pistol would send it bolting for the nearest egress. But the creature seemed to be less skittish, at least compared to previously.

"Hey, little guy," he said one afternoon. "I was thinking you might want to try a little of this."

Moose held out the power-charged alien tech detector slowly. The attacking force's warp power was burned into the piece of wreckage contained within, and even after it had been drained by its previous encounter with the alien, the power had returned to its original levels in short order.

The pink-furred critter paused in its meal, unsure, its large eyes fixing on the device in Moose's hands. It sniffed the air, then somehow pulled power from the device as easily as breathing. Its coat shifted color slightly as it did, taking on a faint golden hue as the warp power drained.

"Okay, fella, that's enough for now," Moose said, standing up to return the device to its storage unit.

The sudden movement made the animal bolt, but it paused at the door, studying the unusual biped that had been feeding it. Then, in a flash of pink and gold, it was gone.

CHAPTER EIGHTEEN

"Are you sure you're ready for this, Holly?"

"I am, Captain. I can say with almost eighty-seven percent certainty that this warp will be successful. And with Ace helping maintain the ship's other systems while I focus on warp, I am quite confident it will be successful."

"I don't mean to rain on your parade, but that's still a thirteen percent probability of shit going tits up," Moose noted.

"Seriously," Hump agreed. "Not to be a downer, but he's right. That's a big window for Murphy to crawl in through."

They both had a point, and it was the same concern Hellatz had mentioned earlier when he and his captain were first informed that the warp system was operational again. They knew the warp had experienced some pretty significant problems, thanks to the alien tech aboard, and then the power-stealing creature that had stowed away. But now it was looking like they could likely engage the system without any significant problems.

Or so they thought. Really, there was no way to know for certain until they tried.

Warp levels were holding steady, though, and when Holly

powered it up to pre-engagement levels, the power didn't surge or fluctuate one bit. Somehow, the alien warp drive was no longer interfering with their own systems.

What they didn't know was the little creature––which Captain Perez had dubbed "Turd" thanks to her first encounter with a trace of it––was snacking on that power, courtesy of Moose. And while he had simply been using the device as a means to lure Turd away from the ship's crucial systems, the unintended benefit was the overflowing warp power was no longer leaking into their own systems.

"We're off-course far from home, and our star charts are corrupted. And even if they weren't, we were thrown so far from our original destination that I wonder if they'd be of use anyway. We need to get back on track, and we need to start logging these new systems. So yeah, thirteen percent sucks, but we need to do this," she told her crew. "So prep your gear. It's going to be a little one to start, but we warp in thirty."

Amazingly, Holly executed the warp to perfection with no problems of any sort arising. They were still far from the nearest system, though, so Sadira had Holly prep for another. And then another. And as many as it would take until they would reach the next star on their trek through the void of space.

"Captain, it looks like there are actually a pair of worlds that might be habitable," Holly informed them when they finally arrived in the sun's orbit. "Unfortunately, too many of my scanning arrays are still experiencing difficulties for me to provide more than rudimentary data."

"Take us toward them, Holly, then hold up in orbit. Hel, Moose, I want you two to take Hel's away ship and go scout it out for us. See what you can find."

"You want Ace to check the other out?" Moose asked. "Two birds with one stone. Or two stones at the same time, I guess."

"No. We still need Ace to maintain too many of Holly's systems to safely disconnect him yet. You two pop out and see what you can see. We'll run a parallel survey from orbit. Hopefully we can get some more of the ship's systems functional enough to get a better reading down there."

"Will do, Cap," Moose said. "You ready, Hel? Just you and me taking a relaxing road trip to a strange new world."

"We are most certainly not going to be relaxing," Hel replied. "And there are no roads required where we are going," he added.

"You're so literal, dude," Moose chided. "Come on, let's get a move on. I'm dying to see what's down there."

"Captain, we shall return shortly," Hellatz said, then followed the cocky human from the command center.

"You want me to go with 'em?" Hump asked. "Given what happened on the last world we set down on and all."

Sadira considered it a moment. A bit of backup might actually be a good thing, and she and Goonara and Ace could handle any little issues that might arise in the short time they were gone. "Yeah, I think that'd be a good idea, actually. Grab your gear and join them. I'll tell them to hold up for you."

"Excellent. Thanks, Cap. This should be fun."

Corporal Humphries hurried off to gather up his gear, then joined his crewmates aboard the little Chithiid away ship. "Okay, you mutts. Let's do this!" he said with a laugh.

Hellatz allowed himself a little chuckle, then gunned the throttle, slamming his passengers into their seats as he popped free of the hangar bay and dove into the planet's atmosphere.

It was a relatively barren world, with sparse forests and areas of vegetation dotting the terrain nearest to water sources, while those in more arid areas were lacking any such plant life at all. Or so it seemed, at least. A hazy mist covered much of the surface, obscuring their regular optical arrays. Mustafa switched over to infrared and made another pass.

"You see that?" Moose asked, pointing excitedly to one of the scanning display screens. "Heat signatures. And lots of them!"

"Indeed," Hellatz agreed, banking the ship for a lower pass.

Corporal Humphries added his own spec-ops scanning arrays on top of those the ship contained, surveying for any traces of dangerous chemical residue, radiation, or other silent-yet-deadly substances. But all came back clear.

"There don't seem to be any cities down there," the soldier noted. "At least, not like we're used to. But there's smoke coming from those caves nearby. The area near that river. You see it, Hellatz?"

"I do," the Chithiid pilot replied. "And it leads me to believe that perhaps this is a primitive, cave-dwelling race."

"That, or it's a subterranean culture," Moose posited. "In any case, there's only one way to find out."

"Agreed," Humphries said. "You good to take us down, Hel?"

"I've already located a suitable landing site," their pilot replied.

Moose leaned in close to the monitors, studying the images slowly becoming more clear as they dropped low for a landing. What he saw was a group of bipedal creatures. But they didn't walk like humans, or even apes. These had hunched backs with what appeared to be spiny ridges protruding from them, the cooler temperatures on the heat scan leading him to believe them to be made of bone or some other material.

"Look at these things," the human gasped. "Captain, you reading this?"

"I am," Sadira replied from orbit.

The aliens were not only tall in stature, but they also possessed broad, muscular shoulders, as well as long, wiry fingers. But these were only infrared images, and until they made actual first contact, what this new species actually looked like was a mystery.

"I'm thinking we need to set down and check this out. You agree?"

"I do," she replied.

"Good, because Hel is already in a descent to a landing zone," Mustafa said.

"Of course he is. Just be careful down there. And if there's any sign of trouble, step back and let Hump do his thing. You ready to rock, Corporal?"

The cyborg patted the pulse rifle in his lap. "Always, Captain."

"Okay. You know what to do. We'll be monitoring you from here, so keep your comms lines active."

"Copy that," Mustafa said, then turned to his shipmates. "All right then, fellas. Let's go meet the locals."

CHAPTER NINETEEN

Hellatz set his ship down in the wide-open clear space between two elevated berms bordered by a sparse growth of thin-trunked trees. It was a conscious decision, not only for its proximity to the heat signatures of the unknown alien species they were about to meet, but it also provided them a three-hundred-sixty-degree view. No one would be sneaking up on them should things go sideways.

The ridge-backed creatures were apparently more primitive than they'd originally expected, their ship seeming to cause quite a stir when it landed. The aliens, despite their intimidating appearance, scattered when the sky vessel descended from above.

"Heat signatures have decreased by fifty percent," Moose noted. "Holly, you seeing anything from up there?"

"The same as you, I'm afraid," the AI replied in his masculine voice. "It would appear a sizable portion of them have retreated into the cave system at the far end of the area you landed in."

"So, big and scary, but really chickens," Hump said. "Typical. It's always the big ones, right, Hel?"

The Chithiid was well aware of his species' height advantage, but he also knew the strange cyborg was just having a little fun with him. One couldn't spend as many years on Earth as he had without picking up on its inhabitants' more colorful quirks.

"Yes, Corporal, it would seem to be the case," he said, then flashed a little grin. "Except when it isn't, of course."

For a Chithiid, Hellatz was something of an anomaly, in that his sense of humor had developed several more human traits over his time with the smaller species.

"You're killing me, Hel," Hump joked as he picked up his pulse rifle and gave it a final check. A little notification ping sounded from the console beside him. The cyborg studied the readout a moment, then turned to his crewmates. "All right, fellas, the air comes back as perfectly breathable. You two ready for this?"

"As ready as I'll ever be," Moose said. "At least these ones don't look like they'll be shooting any pulse weapons at us," he said. "Hooray for primitives, right?"

"Yes. And it's a good thing," Hellatz added as he opened the airlock door. "Had we encountered the advanced race we are actually seeking out, we are in no condition to properly fight, nor flee, if the need were to arise."

"Come on. Enough yapping, you two. It's time to meet the natives," Hump said, then stepped out onto the alien world.

"After you," Moose said with a little bow.

"You are too kind," Hellatz replied, then exited the ship.

The indigenous creatures were even more fearsome-looking in person, Moose thought as the first of the ridge-backed aliens moved toward them from the edge of the clearing. They were carrying clubs and rocks, wary of the intruders in their realm.

"Don't shoot them, Corporal," Hellatz said. "They obviously have no idea what a gun even is, so brandishing it will likely have no effect beyond confusing them."

"Yeah, they're not exactly tactical geniuses, that's for sure," the cyborg said as he slung his rifle and left it hanging at his side. "But if they get rude, I may have to put one down."

"We haven't even said hello yet, Hump," Moose chuckled.

"True. But I've always been one to be prepared."

"Like a Boy Scout, only far more violent," the human said with a laugh.

"The best kind," Hump said with a grin.

"Gentlemen, please. We have company."

"Right, Hel. Game faces, everyone," Hump said as the terrifying-looking natives drew closer.

They were thickly muscled, with sinewy arms and powerful-looking hands, the digits of which each sported a long claw rather than nails. And the protruding ridges they had noted on their approach seemed to indeed be some sort of bone or similar material, they could now see clearly.

The creatures also bore a feature their heat scans had not revealed. A mouthful of sharp, carnivore's teeth, making them all the more terrifying in appearance.

"Hello," Corporal Humphries said, holding up an open hand in greeting. "We come in peace. We mean you no harm."

The creatures let out a shrill clucking sound, punctuated by guttural grunts and squeals. Their language was not what one would call pleasing to the ear.

"You recording, Hump?"

"Yeah. But hearing that, I can't help but think that there's no amount of neuro-stim uploading that'll make sense of that gibberish."

"We've got to try, though. Cap's counting on us."

"I know," he said, taking a step closer, his hands still open and held up at chest level in front of him. "We're friends, see? We aren't going to hurt anyone."

The creatures bellowed at him, a shrieking, horrible sound

that was as much an abuse to his ears as any blow would be to his body. But Hump simply turned the discomfort off. Sometimes, being a cyborg had some pretty distinct advantages over his flesh-and-blood friends.

A trio of vines tied to smooth rocks flew through the air, two of the bolos wrapping him tightly around the cyborg's torso and arms, the third around his legs. Hump turned his gaze to find several of the aliens had popped up from the ground to carry out their attack.

Apparently, there was a more extensive network of caverns and tunnels than they'd anticipated, and they had allowed the natives to flank them without being noticed. The tunnel accessways were covered by woven material that had been covered by dirt and made to blend in to the landscape. It seemed that despite their seemingly primitive nature, the natives weren't as clueless as one might initially think.

More bolos flew, likewise wrapping the human and Chithiid tight.

"I am most definitely *not* amused," Hump said, flexing his cybernetic arms to snap the deep green vines. But try as he might, they wouldn't break.

The sharp-toothed aliens were moving toward them at a quick pace now.

"Very funny, Hump. But seriously, bust us out of here before this gets ugly."

"I can't."

"What do you mean, you can't? You're a freakin' cyborg."

"Yeah, I know, dumbass. But these vines are made of something weird. It's got a higher tensile strength than ceramisteel cable," he said, straining against his bonds. "I'm sorry, guys, but I'm stuck."

Far above, Sadira watched in shock as her team was herded toward the river's edge, where the entrance to a system of caverns was hidden by the shoreline. Once her team went underground, there was a very good possibility they'd lose the signal entirely. As it was, the streams from the Chithiid ship and Hump's uplink were all they had to go on.

"Hey, you guys really don't need to do this," the cyborg said to the nearest creature ushering him and his crewmates toward the dark cavern openings looming ahead. "Seriously, y'all need to stop this."

He received no reply.

Being a spec-ops cyborg, this shit was getting rather old.

"Okay, fuck this," he said, then headbutted the alien beside him while he attempted to get a hand free to grab the pulse rifle pinned to his side.

Six of the burly creatures rushed to their friend's aid, though, and Hump found himself quickly overcome. Without use of his powerful arms or legs, he was simply unable to properly defend himself.

The alien he'd attacked was barking out some gibberish in its language, holding a taloned hand to its face, where the cyborg had apparently broken its nose. The others were not amused.

"What are you doing?" Moose asked the creatures as they tied a large rock around Hump's neck. "Hump, what's going on?"

"Aww, shit," the cyborg replied as they manhandled him toward a deep pool at the river's edge. "Don't forget to get me later," he said.

"Later? What do you mean, later?" Moose asked, just as their friend was pushed off of the edge into the deep waters, his streaming feed going dark as the waters swallowed him up.

"Hump!" Moose called out. "Sonofa..."

"This is a most disconcerting development," Hellatz said.

"No shit. And I think it might be about to get even worse."

The infrared signatures of the last two crewmembers then

disappeared from Holly's scans as Moose and Hellatz were dragged into the aliens' lair.

Captain Perez was at the edge of her seat, her fingers tapping an angry staccato on her console.

"Captain? What do we do?" Holly asked.

"Do?" she replied with a growl. "We go and get them."

CHAPTER TWENTY

Sadira hadn't needed to gear up for a proper fight in ages. Sure, she'd been flying potentially hazardous space missions with Moose for years, but an actual hands-on foot assault? It simply wasn't her thing. That was what they had Corporal Humphries for.

Only he was "indisposed" at the moment. And by indisposed, that meant trapped about ten feet underwater. Fortunately for him, he was a cyborg, and while he may have had a flesh-and-blood covering atop his endoskeleton, he didn't need air to survive.

On top of that, he had a more ruggedized version of human flesh, which meant the limited amount of oxygen stored in his hemoglobin banks was more than adequate to keep it viable for significant amounts of time. Including when he was stuck underwater.

"This really is not my sort of thing," Goonara said as Sadira helped her strap on a pair of pulse pistol holsters and a long combat knife.

"I know, Goonara, but we really don't have an option. Our

people are in harm's way, and we've got no one else to do this but us."

"I realize that," the scientist replied. "It's just that I have never even fired a weapon before. What if I make a mistake?"

Sadira slowed her roll and fixed her crewmember with as kind and understanding a gaze as she could, given the circumstances.

"We're going in to save our friends. And if it comes to shooting, I wouldn't worry too much about it. There are going to be a lot more of them than there are of us. And besides, they've still never seen a gun fire, so I'm thinking that once we open up on them, it should make quite an impression."

"But our people, they will be in harm's way as well," the Chithiid noted.

Sadira was very well aware of that fact, but considering their circumstances, the possibility of friendly fire seemed a far better risk than remaining in the clutches of a race that had shown no hesitation in killing a prisoner, though they had no way of knowing Hump could easily survive drowning.

"Okay, Goonara, let's go over this. I need your eyes and mind to tell me everything you see, even if you think it's trivial. We've gotta find any possible weakness we can. Any weak link. You think you can do that?"

The scientist visibly relaxed at the suggestion. "Yes. I do believe that is something I can handle."

Goonara pulled up the replay of Corporal Humphries' transmission once more and began scouring it for any details that might be of particular use to them as they attempted their rescue. It wasn't until the fourth viewing that she spotted an anomaly that caught her eye.

"Captain, I believe I may have something."

"What is it?"

"Look at this," the scientist said, pointing to the frozen frames just before Hump was pushed into the water. "Their cavern system appears to have multiple entrances. You see this native? It has a distinct scar I noted on the footage during the first moments of the corporal's capture. It is one of the attackers that emerged from underground."

"And? We know they did that."

"Yes, but this one then returned the way it came, while the others took our people prisoner and marched them toward the river."

Sadira saw what Goonara was getting at. "So, that means these little trap doors are actual links to their subterranean network." Gears were turning in her head. It was a little mad, and definitely risky, but it just might work. "Great work, Goonara."

"Do you think this will provide us with any form of strategic advantage?"

"Oh yeah," Sadira replied. "You just gave me a great idea."

Holly entered the atmosphere in a blazing orange-hot streak, directing her descent right at the native creatures' home turf. She had taken on her female aspect for this mission, and she was now bringing death and terror upon the unwitting natives, like a fiery, vengeful Kali come for their heads and hearts. A flying goddess of death.

Her friends were in danger, and she was not about to let that pass.

If the bright craft hurtling toward them hadn't already gotten the cave-dwelling creatures' attention, the sonic boom of her arrival certainly did. These were primitive beings, and a terror from the sky was bound to pique their interest. It was anything but a stealthy approach, but then, it wasn't supposed to be. In fact, the brighter and louder, the better, for Holly was not delivering the little rescue team to the surface.

She was the diversion.

The actual landing had already occurred over an hour prior, the AI ship quietly descending from a distance, then flying low over the treetops until she was near the target zone. She then dropped off her precious cargo and retraced her path before heading back into space to await the signal.

The captain and her science officer would make the last several miles' approach on foot, and even with infrared eyewear to help alert them of lurking hostiles, that piece of tech wouldn't warn them of native booby traps. Those would certainly be made of naturally occurring materials, meaning they would blend in with the rest of the flora they scanned.

They'd simply have to be cautious. There was no way around it. It was exhaustingly slow progress, but the duo eventually made it to the hidden accessways where their friends had been captured.

"Do we really need this many weapons?" Goonara quietly lamented as they walked hunched over in the dim tunnel heading, they hoped, toward their imprisoned friends.

"They're not all for us," Sadira replied. "Once we free our people, they'll increase our numbers, and every additional gun will help improve our odds of escape."

"We certainly brought enough of them," Goonara said, shifting the additional weight of the pulse rifle and pair of pistols slung around her body.

"And if we can get our people freed up and out through the tunnels before they realize what's going on, we might even avoid a fight."

"Do you think that is likely?"

Sadira chuckled in the dark. "Nah. This is totally going to be a shitshow."

CHAPTER TWENTY-ONE

The tunnel stretched and wove for a good long while, the passage apparently being infrequently used. Sadira thought it was likely more of an emergency egress type of thing that the locals had used to sneak up on their people. Whatever the case, it was thankfully devoid of natives.

There were also occasional small offshoots from the main tunnel, but they seemed unused, with no signs of recent traffic. Goonara posited that they likely led to similar exit points elsewhere above. For the most part, it seemed the main entry and exit was the cavernous entrance beneath the overhang near the river's edge.

"These are fascinating," the Chithiid scientist marveled as they passed a larger group of the faintly glowing crystals illuminating their way. "I can't tell what exactly is generating the light, but it's not reading as a radiologic signature."

"That's great, Goonara, but we've got slightly more pressing matters at the moment," Sadira said, pushing ahead. "It looks like this thing opens into a larger chamber up ahead, and that flickering light isn't from some funky crystals. That's fire, so stay focused."

"Of course," the scientist said. But the phenomenon was just too great for her to ignore. Her brain simply wasn't wired that way.

Sadira slowed her pace to a cautious crawl as they neared the larger area. The comparatively dim light of the tunnel would hopefully help conceal them from those in the brighter confines of the more spacious and well-lit cavern, but they couldn't be sure. The native creatures might have a highly developed sense of smell, or perhaps extremely acute night vision.

They were going into a hostile situation with far too little information for Sadira's liking, but the circumstances were what they were, and there was nothing they could do about it.

"Hang back a second," Sadira whispered as she peeked out of the edge of the tunnel.

Goonara was glad for the pause, as it afforded her a moment to pause and draw a knife from her pack to pry one of the glowing crystals from the wall. The captain was correct, there was a far more pressing matter at hand, but that didn't mean she couldn't study the phenomenon later back on the ship, at her leisure.

Sadira scanned the chamber, her eyes adjusting to the brighter light. There was not just one fire, but several, the smoke rising to the soot-darkened ceiling, where it swirled like a pacing beast, cornered and enraged, before finding one of the several small gaps in the rock above, allowing it to rise to the surface.

The natives were gathered in small clusters, eating the flesh of some sort of local game they had roasted. It looked similar to Earth's deer, but for the six legs rather than four. A drumstick lover's fantasy, Sadira mused. The creatures may have cooked their meat, but they ate with no utensils, their sharp teeth ripping their food into large chunks, which they greedily gulped down.

One of the fires seemed larger than the others, and she found her attention drawn to it, not only for its size, but also because of the two men bound to a large pole driven into the ground beside it.

"Shit, there they are," she hissed.

"They are alive, then?"

"Yeah, but from what it looks like, I think these bastards may have some disturbing plans for them."

"Plans?"

Sadira watched the creature guarding Moose and Hellatz move close to them, sniffing each with curiosity. It did not appear to be an assessment of the men's choice in deodorant.

"Yeah. I think our boys are on tonight's menu."

"They would *eat* them?" Goonara asked, shocked.

Chithiid came from a world whose vegetation possessed an incredibly high protein content, leading to their almost entirely herbivorous diet. And while many of them did ingest some animal proteins from time to time, the idea of eating an actual person was utterly unbelievable.

"Yeah, it looks that way, and I don't think our guys would appreciate that, do you?"

"Of course not!"

"It was rhetorical, Goon," Sadira sighed. "Anyway, you ready? We're gonna have to go in fast and hot. That means pulse pistols blazing, you got me? Shock and awe, if you know what I mean."

"I believe I do."

"Good. Now, the guns should scare the natives, so don't worry if your aim is off. Just keep them back and distracted long enough for me to get Moose and Hellatz free."

"I will do my best," the scientist replied.

Sadira almost felt bad for her, being thrust into this situation with no training. But circumstances sometimes arose that forced you to grow, whether you wanted to or not, and this was one such occasion. Goonara was going to be getting her baptism by fire today, and her captain was going to do all she could to make sure she came out of it in one piece.

"All right, we get them free, then make for that big tunnel over there. That looks like natural light, so my guess is we're just inside of that overhang by the river. Once we're out, you haul ass for the ship, ya hear?"

"I have excellent hearing."

Sadira just sighed. She could work on the alien's slang comprehension once they were safely in orbit.

"I'm going to hug that far wall. The shadows should give me a little bit of cover. Now, if they see me, I'll open fire. That'll be your cue to light them up. But, ideally, I'll get close to Moose and Hellatz without being seen. If that happens, I'll key you on comms to start the distraction." She unslung two of the weapons Goonara had been carrying and added them to her own. "Now, stay here, stay out of sight, and wait for my signal."

"I will do as you wish, Captain," Goonara replied. "And good luck."

"Thanks, Goon. We'll need it," Sadira said, wasting no time as she ducked into the shadows and began her rapid approach toward the bound duo.

She made good time, staying unobserved as she darted along the periphery. The native creatures were all huddling around the fires, their attention focused on their roasting meals rather than the uninteresting walls of the cave. In a matter of but a few minutes, the stealthy human had made it as close to her crew as she could before being forced into the open.

"Goonara, I'm in position. I want you to open fire in ten seconds, copy?"

"I hear you and copy, Captain."

Sadira unsheathed the knife she'd brought specifically for this mission. It was a gift from Cal before they headed out on their lengthy journey. An incredibly finely ground edged weapon made of some new composite material he'd been working on with the help of Freya and the other AIs with a penchant for invention.

The result of their collaboration was a non-magnetic blade that could be safely used around sensitive electronics yet would also hold its edge under even the most heavy-duty use. And it was sharp. *Really* sharp. But if Hump couldn't break the vines, she found herself wondering if it would be sharp enough.

A bloodcurdling scream filled the air, followed by a rapid-fire barrage of pulse fire that sprayed across the entire cavern, sending the ridge-backed creatures running.

"Damn, Goon." Sadira couldn't help but chuckle as she raced to her unguarded crew.

"Captain, how did you—?"

"Zip it and shoot, Hel," Sadira said as she sliced his restraints, the blade doing its job, but still requiring all the force she could apply. The bond holding his arms split, and she immediately jammed a gun in his hands, then raced to where Moose was tied up, doing the same for him.

"Let me, Cap," he said, taking the knife from her and muscling through the vines around his legs with his powerful arms. "I'll cut Hel free. What's the egress plan?"

"Goonara's driving them away as best she can. We make a run for the cavern mouth, then back to the ship."

"There's a lot of 'em, Cap," he noted. "More than in here."

"Then we run faster," she replied.

Moose nodded once and rushed to free their pilot's legs.

"Got 'em, Goonara. Move for the exit, now!" she ordered over comms.

The Chithiid didn't need to be told twice. She took off at a run, quickly joining the others just as they reached the cave mouth. Their path outside was relatively clear, but the natives were regaining their composure. It was only a matter of time before they pushed back, and when they did, their numbers would simply be too much.

Moose separated from the group and ran for the water.

"Moose!"

"It's okay, Captain. He'll be back," Hellatz said as they watched the man dive into the water without hesitation.

A long time passed without him coming up for air. Too long, Sadira worried. She was just about to jump in and drag him out herself when Corporal Humphries lunged out of the water with an enormous spray. Moose was in his arms, sucking in lungfuls of desperately needed air.

"That thing working?" Sadira asked of his waterlogged weapon.

Hump swung it to his shoulder and blasted one of the alien creatures foolish enough to make a rush at him. "Yep," he said with a wry grin. "Nice to see ya, Cap. What's the plan?"

"Get the fuck out of here, that's the plan."

"My favorite," he replied. "Come on, Moose. Man up, I'm not carrying you the whole way."

Moose, for his part, was fine now that he had fresh air in his lungs. He handed his captain her knife, which she promptly sheathed, then they took off at a run for their ship.

"I had Holly set down just ahead. Hellatz, we'll have to come back for your ship once we've had a chance to regroup," Sadira said as they raced through the trees. "The ship's right through these—"

They burst from the tree line at a sprint, racing toward the ship. But something was wrong. And that something was the roughly hundred angry native creatures blocking their way, teeth bared and talons ready for a fight.

"Shit," Sadira said, as more of them moved in from the trees at their sides, boxing them in.

"Cap?" Moose asked.

"I'm thinking," she replied.

She was thinking all right. Thinking just how much trouble they were in.

CHAPTER TWENTY-TWO

"Hooooly shit. We are so screwed," Moose said as he scanned the angry, wicked-toothed creatures' faces blocking their path to the ship. "I gave up trying to count how many there are."

"One hundred eighty-seven," Hump noted, his eyes scanning the masses.

"Showoff."

"No. Cyborg," he replied with a little chuckle.

"Still a showoff," Moose shot back. "In any case, that's way too many for the five of us, even with pulse weapons."

He let off a few rounds into the trees to make a show of force and perhaps buy them a bit of time. The leafy tops burst into flames from the impacts, but unlike their flight within the caverns, the indigenous enemy was merely further enraged by the display.

"I don't think that worked nearly the way you intended it to," Goonara said.

"Gee, ya think? Thanks, Goon. If you've got a better idea, I'm all ears," Moose replied.

The creatures were getting antsy, bellowing and stomping their feet as they worked themselves up into a battle rage.

Mouths foamed, and sharp fangs snapped as their aggression increased.

"Oh, this is bad," Sadira said. "I think we need to retreat to the—"

"Not an option, Captain," Corporal Humphries said, his casual demeanor replaced by a far more serious one. The one reserved for combat. The one Sadira had hoped she'd never have to see.

She turned to look behind them. Sure enough, even more of the enemy had begun filtering through the trees. They were cut off and surrounded.

A handful of either particularly brave or particularly foolish natives rushed the intruders.

"Do we shoot them?" Moose asked, showing an unusual amount of restraint.

"I think that would just rile up the others even more," Hump said. "We've gotta do this old-school."

"Shit."

Sadira, Moose, Hump, and Hellatz formed a loose ring around Goonara. She might have figured out how to fire a pulse pistol, but hand-to-hand combat was simply not her forte, and it wasn't something she could fake. They'd have to take on the attackers themselves, while keeping her safe.

The attackers had a bit of a size advantage, their broad shoulders and long talons giving them the appearance of the upper hand. But the four defenders had something the natives didn't have. Martial arts training. While none were as proficient as Hump—who, as a Special Forces cyborg knew more about fighting than they ever would, even with a neuro-stim—all had more than a little training. And against an enemy relying on brute strength rather than finesse, they were actually likely to come out on top. At least against the first few. After that, however, it would be an ugly melee, and one they couldn't hope to win.

Hump dropped the nearest attacker with a brutal punch, putting all of his ceramisteel endoskeleton's substantial force behind it. Hellatz, likewise, threw powerful blows with all four of his arms, overwhelming his assailant as he pummeled him with no restraint.

Sadira and Moose were forced to rely on more conventional fighting styles, leaving them actively engaged with the enemy combatants in a far more heated fight, while the remaining creatures swarmed the Chithiid and the cyborg.

The captain had studied fighting as a hobby on their many missions, and she was morbidly thrilled that the wealth of neuro-stim-implanted knowledge was finally getting a chance to be used. She just hoped it would work.

She dodged a violent attack, the alien's sharp teeth and claws finding nothing but air where she had just been. Her fists, while small in comparison to the creature, nevertheless caused much damage as she unleashed a flurry of punches, followed by a pair of low kicks to the native's knee and thigh, dropping it low enough for a jaw-breaking elbow.

Moose was also faring relatively well and had managed to dodge the swiping talons of his attacker, but not before a slash opened on his shoulder.

"Ow! Sonofa––"

Across the clearing, the ship's lower airlock door abruptly began cycling open.

"What the–? Who's opening the door?" Sadira asked.

"I am," Holly replied over comms.

"Holly, what are you doing? These things can't be allowed to get into the––"

The door opened all the way, and a small, high-pitched howl emerged from the opening.

"What the hell––?" Sadira asked aloud.

The alien monsters were apparently wondering the same

thing. All of them, even those engaged in the fight, turned to look at whatever this strange new thing might be.

A small, fluffy, pink creature strode out of the open airlock, its fur standing on end, making it look larger than it actually was. Even so, the little fur ball was comically small compared to the looming creatures with their bony-ridged backs and massive teeth. It looked at Moose and saw the blood seeping through his shirt and let out an angry growl. Someone had hurt the food-giving person, and it was not amused.

"What's it doing?"

"I don't know, Cap, but it looks pissed," Moose replied.

The creatures' shock wore off quickly, and the little pink creature, though small, looked like it would make for a tasty snack for whichever managed to catch it. A large number of the native aliens began charging at it, talons outstretched in their excitement.

"Run, little guy!" Moose called out.

It did nothing of the sort. In fact, it took another step forward toward the rushing horde. Moose was about to call out another warning when the animal's pink fur abruptly began to glow and crackle.

With a surprisingly strong bellow, it discharged a defensive spray of the deadly warp energy it had ingested and stored. It was like an enraged power skunk, only this one didn't leave stinking victims in its wake. This one melted them into puddles of disintegrated meat.

The blast of energy utterly destroyed the nearest alien attackers before they could even react. Those farther back turned and tried to run. And many of them succeeded in fleeing, though they would bear the scars of the encounter for the rest of their days.

Those that had been watching from afar panicked and ran away, shrieking in fear, the carefully aligned numbers scattering to the wind, their prey suddenly the last thing on their minds.

Holly's crew stood stock-still in shock. Even the cyborg didn't know what to make of it.

The little creature relaxed, its fur dropping back down, making it look like its normal self, then trotted over toward them with a spring in its step. It looked up at Moose with those big eyes and rubbed against his leg.

"Is it... purring?" Sadira marveled.

"I——" Moose was saying, when the deadly little creature jumped up into his arms.

The captain stared at the animal. The thing they'd been trying to kill or capture for so long. Moose was scratching behind its ears, much to the little critter's delight. He looked at his captain and knew what she was thinking.

"Sadi, we can't leave it here. Without power to feed on, it'll be defenseless. You know they'll kill it eventually."

Sadira did know that. She also knew what a threat it was to her ship and her crew. Yet, this unlikeliest of hero had done them a solid and saved them from a certain death. She knew it was foolish, but she owed it. At least enough to make them even.

"All right," she relented. "You can bring it with. But it's your responsibility."

"Of course," he replied.

"And we dump it at the first safely habitable world we find."

"Whatever you want, Cap," Moose said as he stared into the animal's affectionate gaze. "Come on, Hel. Let's go get your ship. I don't think they'll try anything as long as this little guy is with us."

Sadira watched the two trot off to retrieve the Chithiid's away ship, shaking her head in disbelief.

"Not the day you expected when you rolled out of bed, eh, Cap?" Hump asked with a grin.

"Not at all, Hump," she replied. "But I'll take it."

CHAPTER TWENTY-THREE

A week of distance between the hostile creatures and themselves had put the crew at ease, and now that their little stowaway was no longer making their systems drain without warning, Holly was able to execute warps with increasing efficiency. They were by no means back to one hundred percent, but it was a marked improvement from their prior condition.

Moose had taken to feeding the strange creature that had previously plagued them a steady trickle of warp power from the alien warp detector. Keeping its levels lowered was a little additional safety that served two purposes. Namely, preventing another mix-up between the incompatible warp powers, and keeping the little energy-eating animal happy.

Goonara, for her part, was having a field day studying the samples she'd collected during their impromptu rescue mission. The glowing crystal was especially interesting, and she would be found in her lab running test after test more often than not, as she reveled in the utterly novel form of energy it seemed to contain.

The ship was in good working order, more or less, though Holly's mind was still fragmented in unpredictable ways that presented themselves without warning. But the ship was flying true, and they were all breathing a sigh of relief as the conflict behind them grew smaller in the proverbial rearview.

"Is that little turd *still* eating?" Sadira asked, rolling her eyes as she entered the ship's galley.

Moose was sitting with the little pink stowaway curled up in his lap, happily chewing on a food cube. "Hey, let her eat. She used a lot of energy saving our asses," he said.

"Oh, so it's a she, now, is it? How'd you figure that out? It's an alien species."

"Well, she's pink, so I figured—"

"Wow, stereotype much?" Sadira snarked back at him with a grin. "Pretty sexist of you, Moose."

"Yeah, sure, Sadi. You know I'm totally a poster boy for insensitive behavior," he replied. "Am I a sexist pig? Am I, Turd?"

Sadira raised a brow. "Oh, you didn't."

"What? You gave her the name."

"Turd is not a pet's name."

"She seems to like it. Don't you, Turd?" he cooed to the animal contentedly resting on her favorite food-giving human.

"Turd, huh?" Sadira said.

The little pink animal looked up at her, batting its large eyes. Without even realizing she was doing it, she began scratching its cheeks, the vibrating happy rumble from within the critter sending a happy tickle up her arm.

"Well, I guess it *did* need a name," she said.

The way Moose looked at her spoke more clearly than words could. In fact, if he were a little boy rather than a grown man, she'd still know his meaning immediately.

"So, you like her?"

"Well, she *did* save our skins," Sadira admitted. "And I suppose giving it a name *does* imply keeping it."

The smile on Moose's face spread from ear to ear. "Really?" he practically chirped.

"Don't get too excited. It's *your* responsibility, Mustafa. That means you feed it. You clean up after it. And you make damn sure it doesn't start siphoning off power from any of my ship's systems. You think you can do that?"

"You're goddamn right I can! Thanks, Sadi," he said with unconstrained joy.

She supposed they had been on their own in space for a bit too long. Sure, they'd have one another's company on those long runs, but neither had formed any sort of affectionate bonds with anyone when they were back home, and the only love between them was the platonic variety.

Having something to pour his love into had given her friend an outlet neither had realized he needed. And as much as it had never even been a blip on her mental radar, it seemed her crew now had a mascot.

And its name was Turd.

Another week had passed, and though Holly had been unable to restore her star maps, in what was looking more and more like a permanent loss of data, at least she and Ace had been able to unlink. She had control of her systems once again, for the most part, anyway, and the ship was firing on all cylinders.

Ace was thrilled beyond his usual chipper nature, going so far as to take several overly enthusiastic survey flights around every new world they came upon. Sadira supposed she could relate. After all, the poor ship was an AI, and as a conscious entity, being stuck aboard Holly without the ability to so much as pop outside for even a minute was enough to drive anyone mad, even an artificial intelligence.

Hellatz had taken his ship along on a few of those scouting runs, keeping Ace company while also maintaining a little watch for his captain. She trusted the AI ship, but she also wanted to be absolutely certain none of Holly's quirks had been passed on to him after so long linked with her.

But all had checked out, and in short order, Ace was off and flying on his own once more.

"I wanted to thank you all for all of the hard work you've put in these past weeks," Sadira said to the crew as they tucked into their dinner.

The food replicators had been functional for some time, but Moose had just gotten his upgrades installed, meaning for the first time since they'd departed Earth, they would be having a proper dessert.

And, much as she had given him grief for his ridiculous sweet tooth needs, Sadira had to admit it was a welcome morale boost.

"It's been a tough run of it," she continued. "But you all have been exemplary in your efforts, and thanks to your diligence, it looks like the ship is finally back to full functionality."

"Almost," Hellatz noted.

"Well, yeah, obviously," she replied with a little laugh. "But you get the gist. But now we have a choice to make."

"*We* have a choice?" Moose asked. "Since when was this a democracy, Cap?"

"Oh, rest assured, it most certainly is not. But this is something you should all weigh in on. You've all earned that right."

"What exactly are you talking about, Captain?" Corporal Humphries asked.

"I'm talking about our mission, Hump. We've overcome our mechanical issues, but we still don't know where we are. Star charts are being constructed anew with every stop we make in every new system, but as for the way home, it's a crapshoot."

"We know, Cap. We're lost. But what does that have to do with this?" Moose asked.

She looked at the faces of the assembled crew. They'd started off as relative strangers. A crew thrown together by circumstance. And they'd overcome incredible obstacles and come out the other side stronger for it. And they were no longer just a crew. They were a family.

And sometimes as dysfunctional as one, she thought with amusement.

"We have a choice here," she said. "We either push on with our mission, or we try to get home. To *find* home."

"But you just said we do not know which way would take us back," Goonara noted.

"I know, Goon. But this isn't about the path itself. This is about the intention. How we think of this mission as we move forward. Now, it's my intention to carry on with our mission, whichever way it should take us, but I'm asking for your input. We're in it deep, and it'll only get deeper."

She scanned her crew's faces, all of them glancing at one another.

"I'm in," Moose said, always her loyal Number One.

"Me too," Corporal Humphries said.

"We do not have much of a choice, anyway," Hellatz added. "Count me in."

"You know I live for exploration and discovery," Goonara said. "Of course, I am with you, Captain."

A warmth filled her belly as she looked at her crew. They were more than just a team. They were *her* team.

"Ace? Holly? You both get a say in this too, you know."

"What else have I got to do?" Ace said. "This is way more interesting than anything back home, anyway."

"I have to agree with my little friend," Holly chimed in. "And until I either retrieve my fragmented charts, or we stumble upon a familiar landmark, the point is rather moot. So, count me in, of course."

Sadira smiled broadly. "So, there it is, then," she said. "Okay, Holly. Fire up the warp drive. The unknown is calling."

PREVIEW: BELLY OF THE BEAST

WARP RIDERS 2

"What's going on? Where are my goddamn navs and guidance displays?" Captain Perez bellowed in the pitch-black command center of her ship. "And why the hell is my stupid hand not working?" she added, rapping her inert cybernetic replacement on the console with a loud bang.

"Everything is out," Hellatz replied from his pilot's seat, all four of his hands frantically trying every possible combination of guidance manipulation to regain some semblance of control.

"What do you mean, *everything*?"

"I *mean,* I have no controls. Zero. No thrust, not even a hint of power. We're floating adrift," the Chithiid replied.

Sadira imagined the expression on the alien's face, his brow furrowed in frustration, and even the extra set of eyes on the back of his head squinting with concern. But that was all she could do. *Imagine.* Because the entire ship appeared to be without power, and they were stuck in the dark.

For a warp core-driven craft, this was decidedly bad.

"Sadi, how can the warp be out?" Moose asked. "It's not like a reactor system. That thing shouldn't be able to go out. Not like that."

"I know. If it did fail, we should have all blown up in a massive explosion of energy," she replied with a grim amusement. "Something must have drained conventional systems and forced a redirect of power. Could your little pet have something to do with it?"

"She was up here with me," Moose replied. "Not a trace of anything out of the ordinary. Hey, where is she, anyway?"

He was referring, of course, to his little pink-furred friend. A stowaway creature they had come across in the earliest days of their misadventure. An animal with the unusual penchant for absorbing energy, which, while under control now, had proven most dangerous in the not-so-distant past. And now, rather than being tossed out the nearest airlock, she was the unlikeliest of pets. One he had dubbed Turd.

The name was more of a curse hurled by the captain on more than one occasion as they hunted the little animal, but it had amused Moose to no end, and when the creature decided, much like a cat, to call the people aboard its own, the name just stuck.

Now she was an official part of their little crew. A mascot who had saved them all when she sprayed out the energy she had absorbed, literally melting the alien creatures threatening her new food-givers.

From that day on she had truly been one of them, receiving all of the food, cuddles, scratches, and occasional helpings of rechargeable power cells to satisfy her craving for energy in a way that didn't put their entire ship at risk.

Early on, she had unwittingly pulled power from vital systems, including the warp drive. But since they'd been providing her those power snacks, there'd been not a single incident. Until now. But this was something different, and they all sensed it.

A flicker of light illuminated the bridge. A crackle of glowing power in the shape of a ball of fur, floating in the zero-G environment.

"There you are," Moose said, quickly unbuckling his harness and pushing off from his seat. Unfortunately, he pushed off awkwardly as he found his metal replacement leg was also offline. "Shit, my leg's out too," he said, lifting his shirt and sliding his hand into his waistband to the metal hip to open the tiny panel to access the limb's hard reboot.

"What the hell are you doing?" Sadira barked. "Back in your seat, Mustafa. That's an order."

"Just a sec, Cap. I've almost got her."

"*Now*, Moose. Shit is hitting the fan with serious velocity, and I need you at your post."

Her Number One flew true in the weightless environment, all of the years he and his captain had spent out on survey missions searching for intelligent life had given him more than enough time playing in zero-G for it to be as natural as walking at this point.

He twisted in the air—now that he had his bearings in the compartment, thanks to his faintly glowing pet—and planted his feet on the far bulkhead. His leg was powering back up, though it wasn't anywhere near full capacity yet. But it was enough to maneuver. He reached the far wall and pushed off gently and sent himself on a trajectory right back toward his point of origin, namely, his seat, reaching out to scoop up their furry companion as he did.

"Got her," he said as he wrapped the little creature in his arms mid-flight, her diminutive size not even affecting his course.

"Good. Now strap in. We can't afford to have you go crashing into Lord knows what if the gravity systems suddenly reboot. Which is your job right now, by the way."

"I know. I'm on it, Cap," he said as he grabbed the handle on his seat and swung himself and his glowing cargo into place and secured the harness. He gently looped one of the straps over Turd, holding the critter securely in his lap. It was her safe place, and she had no desire to go anywhere else.

Fortunately, her reaction to the dark had provided them a modicum of illumination, though all that achieved was confirming that all of the systems were down.

"Holly? What's our status?" Sadira asked the ship's massive AI.

There was no reply.

"Holly? Can you hear me? Humphries? Goonara? Ace?" Sadira said into her non-responsive console. "Moose, check the comms lines, Holly isn't responding."

"And we are still without propulsion or navs," Hellatz added.

"One thing at a time, Hel. We're in the middle of space, it's not like we're going to crash into anything."

"You hope," the Chithiid snarked. Coming from one of his rather stoic race, the sarcasm was still something of an anomaly to get used to.

"I know. But having Holly back online is priority. She can power up the drive systems and access the external sensors and video arrays far faster than we can."

The three of them worked frantically, attempting to reactivate any systems they could from their darkened stations. Some controls had begun to give off faint light. Systems were powering up, although at a bare minimum of power.

"Good news. Life support has stabilized," Moose called out.

The captain's concern flashed hot. "I didn't know it hadn't been stable in the first place. Our backups and redundant systems should have kept that all on priority-one energy diversion."

"Oh, I know. But it looks like *everything* went out. That's just the first to kick back on," Moose replied.

"No drive systems or navigation, though," Hellatz noted. "And from what I can tell, Holly is offline."

Sadira felt the knot in her stomach tighten. For the massively powerful AI that ran their ship to be powered off meant whatever had happened had been more than a little glitch. Holly was supposed to be immune to that sort of thing.

The alien warp detector that had scrambled the ship's systems was safely tucked away in the cargo hold, and her AI processor cube was well shielded and possessed myriad backup systems, all designed to keep her up and running no matter what.

Apparently, that wasn't the case today.

"Moose, any luck on that damage reporting?"

"None so far."

"And besides the basic life support, any data on our other systems?"

"Again, a big zero," he replied.

Sadira furrowed her brow as she tried to come up with some sort of plan that would keep them from either suffocating, freezing, or blowing to bits from warp containment failure when —if—things fired back up again. She shook her dead hand, feeling the slightest of sensations when the nerve relay reconnected as it began to power up again. The metal fingers were still sluggish, but at least they were responding.

"Hel, how much power do you have in your console? I see systems receiving flickers of power again," Sadira asked.

"Just a tiny bit. Not enough to engage any propulsion. The warp core is still offline, along with secondary power generation."

"Shit," she groaned.

"What do you intend to do about this, Captain?" he asked.

"Gimme a minute here."

"Do we have one?"

"Whether we like it or not," she replied. "Okay, first things first. Moose, I need you to head to the forward airlock. Suit up and get out there. You'll have to decompress it manually and use the emergency crank to open the doors, but we need a quick EVA to evaluate the status of our ship."

"What about the others?" Hellatz asked. "We have still not heard from Goonara or Corporal Humphries."

"They'll have to wait. The ship's dark, but life support's working, so at least we've got that in our favor," the captain replied.

Mustafa unfastened his harness and pushed over to his captain's dimly lit silhouette. The power from her console was minimal, but even that tiny bit of illumination had been a godsend in the previously pitch-black chamber.

"What are you doing, Moose? You need to get to—"

"Here," he said, thrusting the faintly glowing ball of fur. "Keep an eye on her."

"Are you fucking kidding me, Moose?"

Even in the dim light she could see his expression, and it was actually a serious one for a change. "She eats power, Sadi. And she's scared. That's a bad combination on its own, but you've seen what happens when she gets riled up."

Indeed she had, and it had been both amazing and horrifying. Like an angry skunk spraying deadly energy, leaving puddles of flesh in its wake.

"Okay, good point," she reluctantly agreed, taking the warm and gently vibrating creature into her lap. "Just behave, you hear me?" she said, giving Turd a little chin scratch.

The pink-furred critter looked up at her with its big gray eyes, the vibrating increasing as it settled as close to her body as it could. The zero-G setting made it difficult to snuggle, but damn if the little animal wasn't doing her best in spite of it.

"Hey, I've got a little power here," Hellatz called out excitedly. "Not much, but I think if we tag-team the controls we might be able to get a bit of thrust."

Sadira turned her focus back to the console in front of her. "Moose, get moving, and take the hard-line spool out there with you to communicate directly. We'll need solid connection since the wireless comms appear to be toast."

"You sure you're not just having a stroke?"

"Ha-ha. Get moving."

"Already gone," he replied, grabbing the coil of comms wire kept for emergency situations and plugging it in then pushing off for the door.

Moose put all of his experience in weightless environments to good use, floating effortlessly out the command center door while pivoting and grabbing the frame as he passed. His body twisted mid-flight, and he planted a foot on the wall, then thrust himself down the corridor, flying like the unlikeliest Superman, albeit with no cape or unitard.

He rounded the corners quickly, redirecting in the darkness with ease. While he hadn't spent nearly as much time aboard this ship as the one he and Sadira had lived aboard for the past several years, he had more than enough time to become quite familiar with its layout in their short time aboard.

Again, he rounded a corner by touch alone, pushing off hard after ensuring the spool of comms wire wasn't tangled.

"Holy crap!" he nearly screamed as he bumped into the floating body of a man.

"What is it?" Sadira demanded over his open comm line.

Moose shined his portable light on the drifting body of their cybernetic crewmate, his eyes open but unseeing. "It's Hump. He's floating out here; seems totally deactivated."

"Damage?"

"None that I can see."

"Then he can wait. Get moving. We need to know what the ship's status is."

Moose pushed the man's bulk aside and continued down the corridor to the airlock he would be using. The locker of space suits was next to it, and donning one was second nature by now, even in the extreme darkness. He could have used his light, but at the moment it made sense to save every bit of power possible, just in case.

"Okay, the suit has power to life support, so I'm heading out," he said a few minutes later, after plugging the comms line into his suit's helmet. "Confirmed, power is out to the airlock. I'm manually cranking the doors open."

"Copy that. Be careful out there."

"Will do."

Moose popped the panel in the wall open and pulled the manual release lever, then folded down the hand crank and began slowly opening the airlock's inner door. It was fairly quick work as the pressure was the same inside the chamber as the ship.

He then performed the reverse once inside, carefully re-patching his comms connection into the wall adapter and allowing the door to seal.

"Depressurizing," he announced as he manually spun the valve venting the chamber's atmosphere into space. It was a relatively quick process, so he began cranking the outer door lever almost immediately.

The thick hatch slowly slid open until there was finally enough space for him to crawl out. He re-patched one more time, reconnecting to the socket just outside the door. Once outside, he immediately cranked the hatch shut, protecting the ship from risk of any decompression accident, just in case. Then he crawled along the ship's hull to determine what, if anything he could see.

"Moose, status."

"Just pushing out over the hull, Cap. The ship looks good. I don't see any leaks, but external illumination seems to be out across the whole ship. I think we've maintained an atmospheric seal."

"Finally, some good news," Sadira said.

"Yeah, tell me about it," Moose replied, his gaze drifting to the stars floating in the inky blackness all around them. His breath abruptly caught in his throat. "Oh, *shit*," he gasped.

"What is it? Sitrep!"

He struggled to find the words. "Uh, Captain? You're not going to believe this."

ALSO BY SCOTT BARON

Standalone Novels

Living the Good Death

The Clockwork Chimera Series

Daisy's Run

Pushing Daisy

Daisy's Gambit

Chasing Daisy

Daisy's War

The Dragon Mage Series

Bad Luck Charlie

Space Pirate Charlie

Dragon King Charlie

Magic Man Charlie

Star Fighter Charlie

Portal Thief Charlie

Rebel Mage Charlie

Warp Speed Charlie

Checkmate Charlie

The Space Assassins Series

The Interstellar Slayer

The Vespus Blade

The Ghalian Code

Death From the Shadows

Hozark's Revenge

ABOUT THE AUTHOR

A native Californian, Scott Baron was born in Hollywood, which he claims may be the reason for his rather off-kilter sense of humor.

Before taking up residence in Venice Beach, Scott first spent a few years abroad in Florence, Italy before returning home to Los Angeles and settling into the film and television industry, where he has worked as an on-set medic for many years.

Aside from mending boo-boos and owies, and penning books and screenplays, Scott is also involved in indie film and theater scene both in the U.S. and abroad.

www.ingramcontent.com/pod-product-compliance
Lightning Source LLC
Chambersburg PA
CBHW022030170626
46808CB00003B/1134